The Women Who Loved John Benson

The Women Who Loved John Benson

William Flagg Magee

The Women Who Loved John Benson

Published by William Flagg Magee

© 2013

CONTACT:

William Flagg Magee
q7photo@mageeimagesllc.com
214-577-9490

Dallas, Texas

FIRST EDITION

ALL RIGHTS RESERVED. No part of this book may be reproduced in any form or by any means whatsoever, including photography, xerography, broadcast, transmission, translation into any language, or recording, without permission in writing from the publisher. Reviewers may quote brief passages in critical articles or reviews.

Printed in the U.S.A.

Cover photo taken by William Flagg Magee
at Valley House Gallery, Dallas

ISBN: 978-1-62847-251-6

www.Q7PHOTO.com

Acknowledgements

I would like to express my thanks to the following:

My wife, Sally, for her patience, support, encouragement and love, and for being at my side for over thirty years

I am grateful to my ancestors. Without them I would not have had the gene pool and artistic heritage they handed down.

To the people who read sections of the manuscript, providing helpful criticism:

Mary A. Burnham for reading sections and introducing me to people who fired my creative energy. Geena Rose DiGiovanna, thank you for clearing the obstacles blocking my creative instincts, and Beverly Davis, PhD for the awareness to appreciate the Talents I have been given.

Prologue

The Learjet was backed out of the hangar, engines started. The pilot, Steve Chappelle, contacted Las Vegas Ground Control.

"Las Vegas Ground, this is Learjet 24, November 713 Mike Alpha Bravo. Permission to taxi to takeoff."

"Seven-thirteen Mike Alpha Bravo, taxi to runway 18 left, hold short. Incoming three miles."

"Roger that, hold short Mike Alpha Bravo."

The Southwest 738 flew by. Steve Chappelle heard its main gear squeak as rubber and concrete touched.

The air traffic controller's voice crackled through Chappelle's headset, talking to a Southwest pilot who had just landed. "Southwest 2172, take the high speed right and proceed to your gate."

The Southwest captain acknowledged. "Roger, good day."

To Chappelle, the controller said, "Learjet 713 Mike Alpha Bravo, position and hold."

"Roger, position and hold."

Chappelle lined the Learjet on the centerline of the runway, advancing the throttles to half power. Applying more pressure on the brakes, the small jet quivered.

"Learjet 713 Mike Alpha Bravo, you're cleared for immediate takeoff. Contact Departure Control frequency 121.06, squawk 7200."

Chappelle repeated, "One-twenty-one point zero six. Squawking 7200."

The Learjet 24 screamed down the runway, lifting quickly into the hot afternoon sky. Chappelle retracted the gear and flaps. Following the air traffic controller's instructions, he turned the plane right and started the Learjet's climb.

Chappelle reached for a small lever next to his left knee. He flipped it up to release the contents of the container. As the plane reached 15,000 feet and turned to its assigned heading, he smelled something strange. Looking over his right shoulder he noticed a hazy substance moving forward from the aft section of the fuselage.

The air controller squawked in Chappelle's headset, "Learjet 713 Mike Alpha Bravo, contact Flight Control on 126.95."

Chappelle panicked. He coughed and breathed in air that had a faint, metallic taste. He evaluated his situation. He knew that as soon as the plane's wheels had left the ground a large sum of money was wired into two accounts on the Isle of Mann. He also knew he was a dead man. The thought of killing thousands of innocent lives made him feel sick. Chappell knew about the Sheik's plan of utilizing the canister to disperse the Ebola bacteria. The money Chappelle was offered would secure his family's future beyond his children's lifetime.

"Oh Lord, what have I gotten myself into?" In a sobering moment, he suddenly decided not to go through with this. "How the hell am I going to find a solution?"

Las Vegas Air Traffic Control was busy trying to contact him.

"Shit." Steve accidentally hit the microphone button.

"Lear 713 say again . . . Lear 713 Mike Alpha Bravo, do you read?"

"Roger."

"Seven-thirteen Mike Alpha Bravo, climb to and maintain Flight Level 390. Turn to and maintain heading 020 degrees."

"Roger FL 390, 020 degrees." Chappelle clicked the microphone button twice.

He recovered and glanced over his right shoulder a second time, hoping he had seen an apparition. What he now saw was gas escaping from one of the lines leading to a canister full of Ebola. A dose of Ebola virus engulfed him.

Then Steve Chappelle took a breath, one of his last. He said, "What to do?" He knew his response to Air Traffic Control was a temporary fix. Where was he? He was at that moment skirting the terrain about fifty miles west of Groom Lake.

He couldn't declare an emergency, turn around or just open a door and air out the cabin. He thought of a plan that would end his misery and hopefully destroy the live bacteria.

He was passing through 34,000 feet. He turned off his transponder and radio, and dove straight for the highway heading north out of Las Vegas to Mercury. As he dove he used Mt. Charleston as a shield. Skimming the tops of sagebrush, he headed towards the western slope of the mountain, avoiding radar contact.

Air Traffic Control noticed contact with November 713 Mike Alpha Bravo was lost. Radar showed the plane changing altitude and direction.

The Nevada Test and Training Range was notified.

Chappelle had the little Learjet flying directly over the flat land paralleling the highway on the western slope of Mt. Charleston. Radar could not find him. Time was precious.

He pulled the nose up to gain altitude. The little jet responded to the slightest touch. He had seen lots of maps of the area and knew where he had to go. He just hoped he had enough time.

He flew into and around the canyons surrounding the Range. The hills were iron red, hot, dry, inhospitable. He then climbed to 2,500 and turned east and again headed for the deck. Over the top of the second canyon ahead was Groom Lake. "Might as well have some fun." He topped the second canyon, bursting over Area 51. He flew down the centerline of the longest runway he had ever seen.

Air Force F-15s, alerted by their radar, turned towards him.

Chappelle applied full power and put the plane in a steep climb.

On the ground F-15s hurtled down the runways. The Lear 24 could out climb an F-4 Phantom through 10,000 feet, but Chappelle was headed as high as the Lear could go, hoping to gain the frigid air of higher elevations.

One fighter turned left, the other right and both fell in behind the Learjet. Not wanting to close too quickly, the fighters made two "S" turns, lined up and loosed two missiles. They were finished. Chappelle saw the missiles coming and closed his eyes, and said a final prayer.

* * *

The fiery ball that once was the Learjet 24 arched upward, momentum carrying it higher. The plane was engulfed in flame. Explosions and subzero temperatures snuffed out whatever life had been on board. The wreckage corkscrewed and fluttered to the ground.

Part One

John Benson

Chapter One

As John Benson walked through his office, the TV was on. The chatter coming from CNN was a welcome distraction. Helicopter video of the wreckage of a plane crash came on the screen, demanding his attention.

Being a photojournalist, news traveled at light speed to his smart phone. Scanning the text message, John quickly learned about the crash of the Learjet, as well as of the dead Ebola bacteria. It was just another sign that John Benson's world was falling apart.

The plane crash triggered a search involving Israeli and American Intelligence Agencies, the Mossad and the CIA. It would be a big story, perhaps one that would get his photos published in a national magazine. The story was John's if he wanted it. But he had other, more personal matters to deal with. Pieces of his life to put back together. He responded to his boss, suggesting another photojournalist take the story. John sat in his chair as he took in the weight of everything that had happened in the past two months. He had endured two back-to-back deaths. His mother had passed away two months prior, and now the tragic death of his wife, Mimi. He mourned both, but mourning his wife exposed emotions he had never before experienced or and brought up memories long forgotten.

Unable to look at the crash footage any longer, he picked up the phone, called the funeral director, and continued the numbing task of preparing for his wife's funeral.

As John walked through the cemetery where his mother was buried, he was connected to his thoughts. Walking connected him to that mysterious realm that is invisible to the human eye. As he passed each gravestone, he felt like spirits were watching him. Scattered about the cemetery were maple and oak trees. On this autumn day the leaves were at their colorful best. But he knew this beauty was only temporary. Leaves burst into beautiful colors only to fade, die and fall lifeless to the ground. He meditated on the fallen leaves. Death was on his mind. The paradox of death because it was through both of their deaths, his mother's and his wife's, that he had learned about himself and about God's unfailing existence.

Death is the gateway to eternal life. Death is a beginning not an end. Death both slays and moves mountains within one's self that builds pathways to life, love, joy and humility. Our failings may be called by many names, but it is our denial of them that builds layers to keep life at bay, and it is the frailty of those layers that allows mortal defects to run rampant.

Morning comes and mourning follows quickly. Death transforms one truculent relationship into a relationship of mutual love and respect. Death steals another. Mourning comes. Mourning is stealthy. Mourning stays a long time.

Death and mourning can screw up a perfectly lovely morning, John Benson thought.

It was the plane crash that made him consider the effect of death. He was not alone. John Benson didn't know, but his best guess was that in order to inventory his emotions, change must happen. Change can be frightening. The fear of change was all too familiar to him. Embracing the unfamiliar emotions erupting from his own denial paralyzed him.

"Aha! There is hope." Embracing his own fear freed him from its grip and power.

He stopped and looked at the fall sky through a canopy of green, red, yellow and brown leaves. Humbled by the beauty surrounding him, he took several deep breaths, looked around, looked up and set off again.

People often speak of miracles. Miracles of death and renewal are taken for granted. Fall colors and spring blossoms are admired and expected to appear twice a year.

His footfall released his mind. He had seen animals die, even participated in their deaths. People are different. Witnessing the process and appreciating the processes of human death is different. Tragic, sudden, violent death, birthed by capricious, malevolent acts is another death. Sudden death leaves a hole. Witnessing death with dignity is a privilege.

God demands accountability. The process of accountability is painful, humiliating. Perhaps God is really like the Fram oil filter man: "Pay me now or pay me later."

When I know for sure I'll let you know, John thought.

The question he imagined was not *How am I going to square the deck?* but rather, *How does God want me to get square with everyone?* It was never too soon to begin. He didn't wish to be like one of the Maidens in *the New Testament* story and be locked out when the party started.

When his mother was in the hospital shortly before her death, John had asked her if the words she wrote were the window to her soul. She beamed. No words could replace the smile on her lips and the light in her eyes. He told her he had found the mother for whom he had been searching all his life. The connection was made. They rejoiced. She was ready.

She had written a poem about a lover mourning a lovers' quarrel. The imagery, the passion, real and intense, he could see the young woman standing at the banister rail looking to the entryway below. She hears the door open and sees the man enter. She imagines what it would be like to fly down the stairs on sandal-clad feet to be swept into his arms, feeling the back of his neck against her bare arms as their lips come together.

The intensity of that image staggered him. The telling came from knowing what that neck felt like as her arms caressed it. That was the same passion and life force of a woman who loved. She brought the same passion and life force into every facet of her life. John remarked that the speck of time they had shared as mother and son made the truculence of fifty years seem like a gnat bite on an elephant's side. Today, right now, that gnat bite was much larger than the elephant.

I have, he thought, *an appreciation for this mystical connection.*

He remembered his mother in the Big House with the smell of leather and pinion wood sitting before the fire, her 1949 Ford with the wood sides. Memories that transcend a lifetime, and in which the bitterness felt in their world had been obliterated by the miracle of reconciliation and transformation.

He looked at the shadows beginning to lengthen. He imagined Mimi, his late wife, being with him on days like this one. The sun was at his back and low in the sky. The trees began to take on different shapes and hues. He stopped to look at what he would come to remember as the most beautiful fall afternoon he'd ever seen.

Then he realized something was wrong with the picture he had painted. What was wrong was that he had been absent from the picture. He had the sickening awareness that instead of being present, he just floated through life.

He remained detached from the feelings swirling within him. He might as well have been locked in a clear sphere set loose on the currents. Frantically he looked around for someone to blame. He was alone. He wanted someone to blame, to shift the awful reality so he wouldn't feel the sickening emptiness in his stomach. The cavern in his gut pushed him to a place so vile and revolting he wanted to run. But he was running, but not outrunning the awfulness encompassing him. When would it stop? What would he have to endure?

Endure! Endure! The word flew through his brain and began racing around every neuron, synapse, and flung itself into the pit of his existence. Lurid memories flooded his mind. Vivid images of the accident that killed Mimi clicked through his mind like a disturbing power-point presentation. He thought of his mother's last days in the hospital. She had been dying as her body, damaged from too many horses landing on it, combined with the hard life fifty years on a ranch will contribute, simply gave out. Simultaneously images of the crumpled Learjet came into focus.

John said to his mother's gravestone, "The thing you feared more than facing those stuffed-away memories came to visit. Death paid you a visit. Death was not for you. It was for others. Before death could have the last dance you had to become accountable. You and God working things out in the private sleep of the soon-to-die."

As the venom spewed out he realized that in the end there had been reconciliation and transformation for both. They found what they had been looking for: He a mother, she a son.

John Benson reflected upon interactions with a psychologist who came to him through one of those people mysteriously placed in his life. John was aware of generational garbage that all children carry around. Some carried their parents' baggage longer than others, some unaware of those wounds.

His awakening came when he spoke with the woman about seeing the total picture of his relationship with his mother. He knew he could not just focus on the four months their relationship had been transformed from hate to love. From go away to come here, to for over fifty years, to a real mother-son relationship.

The psychologist had said, "Be honest with the reality of all that has happened."

The feelings coming from within him that afternoon were more honest than he had ever been about her abandonment and abuse. The barrier he built at age five to protect himself from the hurt she had caused finally crumbled. The honest admission of retribution he succeeded to inflict upon her brought shame. She, before she died, had forgiven him and he her. The image was clear and clean. Those scars she tried to heal by doing to him what had been done to her were healed. One parented as one was parented. The truculent issues they inflicted upon each other went far beyond generational issues. They were cultural. The collective unconscious went more than several generations back. The gene pool John possessed was more than three or five or ten generations back. He had genes from the very first ancestor in his lineage. Cultures that each generation experienced were within John's genetic pool. Perhaps the most immediate generations had the most affect upon the inner man, but there were those long ago, unknown relatives, whose genes became just as dominant as parents, grandparents, great-grandparents. John knew he was free from the violent truculence of the relationship with his mother. He dropped the bag of boulders he'd been carrying all his life. Mother and son were free. But for John, there was no moment of peace. His anger and rage became a deep sadness.

His heart turned its attention to his dead wife. Vivid memories of his beloved Mimi took his breath away.

"Why? Why?" he asked the sky.

John couldn't stop the tears. His dear, loving, creative Mimi was gone. He felt so alone.

Chapter Two

The illusion men and women see in each other can be a train wreck waiting to happen, sometimes not. There was no illusion in what John Benson saw in Mimi—kindness, toughness, intelligence; she had had genuine love for him. She had seen in him a handsome, rough-cut diamond. He had presented a challenge. She could not resist the challenge he presented. They had come from similar backgrounds; came from not-too-old money and shared an interest in the outdoors, photography, the arts and each other. Each found the other wildly sexy and exciting. They saw their lives melding into one big exciting life. Life has other plans, though, and as the wedding day became more than just a distant speck on the horizon, Mimi subtly and smoothly began to infiltrate John's life. She didn't take over; she simply, subliminally made changes John thought were his own ideas. And they were good.

There are exceptions to everything. Every man, woman and child has sometimes subtle, sometimes glaring character defects. The English professors will ask students to point out a character's "fatal flaw", which when one looks for a fatal flaw is sometimes difficult, at first. But if the same teacher asked his charges to point out a character's defects of personality as nearly resembling their own, how many flaws might a character have? One tends to be blind to one's own defects; their answers might originate in the flaws they perceive in their classmates, or their parents or siblings. The point, again a generalization, is that men don't think they have any flaws, of any kind. John was no different. At the time, he had been young, well-educated, well-off, well-connected, had a good job. He loved his work and pursued it passionately, but not as passionately as he had pursued Mimi. This master of his own universe headed blindly, idealistically towards the altar.

Meanwhile, Mimi, her parents, John's parents, her best friend and the best of her good friends busied themselves planning for the big day. Included in the plan was Mimi's plan to domesticate John. This effort was laid out with the precision of an elegant soufflé, no slamming doors or chilly blasts.

Mimi, too, was well-educated, well-off, and well-connected. Her father was a successful investor in the oil business and involved, to a lesser degree, in real estate and printing. The printing business somehow got pushed into the background. It wasn't seen as a particularly glamorous business. Like milking cows. However a well run printing business could return handsome dividends. Yes, cameras, presses and the like absorbed a good bit of capital, but properly utilized they spit out a lot of capital. Whatever the case, Mimi's father was maybe not "Big Rich", but he came close.

She was well provided for. As customary in that time, one did one's best to give back to the community. Her work was working with less fortunate children, teaching them to read and draw with occasional side trips to museums.

Her mother was kind, almost suffocating Mimi. Her father's drive and success influenced her despite frequent absences. Her mother's family was from the Old South; her father's from the West. Each parent was a product of his or her own regional culture.

Cultural mores leave a large generational genetic imprint on successive generations. *Wild Man to Wise Man* is a book illuminating the reason some parents leave unkind footprints on their children's psyche. Parents parent the way they were parented. Mimi's parents deliberately set about to change festering parental wounds they carried. Both wanted their daughter to be healthy in every way.

Discussing the generational wounds, Mimi's parents decided to investigate their ancestors. They discovered the hardships immigrants from the Scottish Lowlands had endured. These were the stoic pioneers who blazed the trails over the Cumberland Gap, opening the gateway to the Southern Plains. Their stoicism colored every aspect of their lives, their culture, and touched every generation succeeding them. Mimi's parents were trailblazers of a different ilk.

John's father was just as successful, and a good friend of Mimi's father. Both Mimi and John had known each other for a long time, but they acted like acquaintances rather than friends. John's father was successful in the brokerage business. He had a long and very successful career regardless of Bull markets, Bear markets or what seem to be called these days as "market disruptions". Translated, that means the bottom fell out and very quickly and often times violently. He was thick skinned, had a great laugh, and was a wonderful storyteller and loved his wife and only child.

Both John's mother and father came from the Southwest. Neither John nor Mimi nor her brother, Nathan, seemed to have been spoiled. They grew up in a house occupied by long-serving help who loved them as their own. Their father saw to it that their children understood the value of money, hard work, honesty and an ethical base built upon sound principals. The hand was not abusive, used to chastise not punish. Discipline was enforced and explained, not abused. They grew up in loving homes with strict but very loving, caring parents.

They met a few years after graduating from different colleges in different parts of the country. He was an on-the-job journalist working for his hometown paper, and Mimi worked teaching children the importance of books and art. Her work was well received in the community. As her name began to circulate, the paper decided to do a story about her, her work and the progress the children had made. John was sent off with pen, pad and camera to do the story. He walked into the classroom and, recognizing her, began an easy conversation. Too easy, thought Mimi, but as the interview and photographs of the children wound down, she began to see a something—a blurry something in this not so strange, strange young man that softened her first feelings. As he left, he asked if he might return to show her his story, as well as the photographs the paper would use for the story.

She said "yes," and then began to worry if it came out as sounding too eager.

They both had had other love affairs, if that's what they really were. Hearts had been broken, young dreams shattered. Somehow, some way they managed to live through it all and arrive once again at the unfamiliar starting point of a new love affair. Their love affair was to last over thirty years. They had ideas of how a marriage ought to really work. His were obviously based on some male stereotype and hers were far more subtle and effective. John could cook. That was perhaps his saving grace in the first year or so of marriage. Not that he had to feed himself, but if he arrived home ahead of her, he'd cook dinner. This was not a common occurrence, but a welcome one and gave them an opportunity to be together. Conversation without interruptions settled the dust before it had a chance to fly.

After their daughter, Grace, was born, things changed. Mimi "retired". John worked harder. They had discussed the "Great Thorn" of many marriages—money—and shunned an extravagant lifestyle. Yes, there was a country club membership, but no big parties except when to have one made sense. His journalism friends loved to drink and it seemed that any reporter worth his salt drank, heavily. John avoided the bars except when to do so might have been unwise, but he didn't abuse the privilege. As he grew more interested in photojournalism, he weaned himself from writing stories, and, as he did, found he possessed the talent to excel. As his reputation grew so did his income, as well as demands on his time. As dominoes fall, the time he spent at home dwindled; signals were sent suggesting a well-paying mistress was causing trouble.

Men, as a rule, don't read signals wives, girlfriends, or lovers send about through changes in mood and position. Work began to overtake his commitments. Commitments Mimi took as seriously as her wedding vows. It was not as if John had abandoned kith and kin; it, work, travel, glamour, recognition, praise and more money began to seduce him as surely as any woman bent upon seducing him. He lost track of his real priorities. Mimi, sidetracked by his success, patiently lived with his absences. When he was home he was a devoted father, husband and lover. He would surprise Mimi by taking her to lunch at a lovely hotel in a small flower-filled suite. These excursions served to diffuse whatever ill feelings she had had about his being gone, and reassured her she was loved and honored by her husband. They would be entwined to the breaking point. During the pillow talk that followed, they talked about Grace, her plans and his next assignment.

Tangled thighs and tousled hair spoke to the depth of their passion. Regardless of these and other assignations, the breaking point arrived.

Another war, more photographs, one last shot before leaving, and he got shot. Getting shot is not what any photojournalist aims to accomplish in the field, but fortunately the bullet went through his thigh without hitting anything too important. The friendlies carried him to a small field hospital where his wound was treated, bandaged. He was given a handful of pain pills and told to be careful. This was but a prelude to the explosion he would encounter when he returned home; having missed Mimi's parents' 40th wedding anniversary, an occasion of which he was well aware and had committed to attend.

Taking a cab home from the airport, he pondered the meaning of Mimi's tone on the phone, telling him he could get himself home; she'd be busy. He liked the reunions at the airport; made him feel like a conquering hero. He liked arriving on Friday evening and seeing both Mimi and Grace waiting as he got off the plane. Grace was beginning to blossom, grow, change, and the changes from the time he left to returning were noticeable. Her blonde hair was still a white blonde, and her brown eyes seemed larger, and her face was changing from that of a child to an almost teenager. So much for pondering as the cab stopped in front of his house. He paid, went to the front door, let himself in and was greeted by a loud silence. Evidence of a party was at hand and he cringed remembering his broken commitment. Contritely he carried his bags upstairs to the bedroom and began to unpack. The housekeeper, a benefit of his success, greeted him and informed him his wife would be out for the afternoon and not to expect her or Grace for supper.

This was not in his plans, nor his idea of fun. Changing into shorts and T-shirt, John morosely put on his running shoes to go limp around the neighborhood. He closed the door quietly as he left, as if she were napping downstairs.

There are consequences that result from everything one does. Some come later in life in the form of replaced hips and knees, other maladies for which the process began many years before. And then there are consequences that come swiftly and painfully. John knew that the consequences about to befall him were of the latter variety. Breaking a commitment to Mimi carried harsh consequences. There were no missed connections. He'd gotten himself shot, but he kept that to himself. No point getting his family in a lather, besides, he thought, limping into the arms of wife and daughter, the brave, wounded, redound photo journalist would elicit appropriate sympathy and adoration. Bad thought. He also thought the party would be held the day he returned. Maybe he should have had it in his pocket calendar. Bad move there. What if the car he was in had gotten waylaid on his way to the airport? What if, if? No good, face the music, and pray for peace in the world. At that point he'd have settled for Gandhi and Christ for dinner, maybe St. Michael too.

Mimi's car was in the drive when he returned. Taking a deep breath he walked into the house, up the stairs to their room. She was on the phone. She turned and looked at him. Her eyes conveyed a message no words could. Simple question: "How could you have done something so stupid and selfish? What were you thinking? Why did you not call? Christ! You got shot, too. You are selfish and self absorbed beyond all proportion. Why?"

His eyes turned away; his body followed. He felt as if he could, should slither under the rug. His stomach felt hollow, empty, and his self-esteem slipped away. The desert, he was lost in a desert he had created for himself. Wandering in circles he tried to find some mental purchase to get himself started. Nothing came. There was a terrible emptiness; he feared to the depth of his being that he would lose her; lose Grace, lose everything.

Turning away, he prayed to whatever God he hoped would listen, would lift him from the abyss.

"John? John, John!" Mimi called to him. "Answer me, John."

He walked into the bathroom, turned on the cold water and splashed his face. Turning, he walked into the bedroom and looked her in the eyes.

"I have no excuse."

Her eyes, fixed on his, softened, but for a brief moment.

"You've hurt people who love you very much."

"I was wrong."

"Have you no more to say? I'm waiting for a fascinating

story. Give me a good one."

"I was wrong."

"Goddammit John! I want to hear at least one sniveling excuse, one outrageous tale!"

"No excuses, no tales. I was wrong. What do you want me to do?"

"I would just like to hear, for once, a plausible excuse for your breaking a commitment you made to me. You made it the day we were married, and you made it again five years ago when we talked about priorities. I told you then I'd support your work, traveling to God knows where, wondering if you'd do something stupid and get hurt. Well, you've done something both stupid and thoughtless. Now, I'd like to cut off your big brassy balls and have them freeze dried for posterity!"

"Mimi! I was wrong, stupid, whatever. What do you want me to do?" He pulled up a leg on his shorts. "See, something stupid. I got shot. That's not an excuse; it's not a reason. I just was wrong. No excuses."

"Too bad your shooter couldn't have shot higher and to the right."

In the lives of those who truly love, passionately love, the consequences of something omitted produced a sometimes forceful and equally passionate response. Mimi's anger, fueled by the fear that something might really have happened to her lover and anger over his missing her parents' party, boiled into a fury. It had to run its course, and deep down John realized the less he said, the shorter the course, he hoped. Yes, she was concerned about his wound and hauled him, silently, to the doctor. Yes, she loved him, and slept in their bed, although well on her side. In the morning she reached for his and withdrew her arm. John went about his business without trying to appease, butter-up, make light, or otherwise do anything to upset her. They both separately and together did things with Grace, and in doing for Grace did for each other.

John and Mimi went to movies, alone. They laughed, held hands, and he courted her. Courtship moved swiftly to hot kisses, and in their bedroom they undressed each other, slowly, and slowly, deliberately, did those things to each other that excited beyond excitement. They slept in each other's arms.

Chapter Three

The small elegant U-shaped shopping center glowed brilliantly in the winter night. Frosted lights framed its U shape in a Currier and Ives sort of way. Standing at the open end, John watched people move about in colorful winter clothes. His mind floated into some cozy space within itself and he wished he could freeze time. Bring it all back to some hot, sultry August afternoon.

He walked on, holding onto the scene. He kept other memories at bay. Memories of times and places he once thought so important now felt empty as the darkness swallowed him. What was it? How could a shopping center catering to such extravagant, meaningless shallowness—unless one was a consumer of vanities—have such an impact? Mortals had nothing to do with the effect affecting him at that moment. What he wanted more than any of the material treasure on display was a hand, a warm elegant woman's hand with whom to share this moment. His heart ached and the memories descended upon him unmercifully. Maybe Mimi was in the soft delicate glow of the lights, or in the even more delicate crystals of frost. She had been that delicate. But she, his wife, was dead.

The best part of a funeral is before it's held. People, family, good friends, well-meaning friends and acquaintances and the clergy keep one occupied. There are, if not already done so by the decedent, plans to be made. Hymns, prayers, Bible verses, who reads what and in what order. The service is distracting enough, in a good way, but tears and memories burst forth not only from within, but from both good and well-meaning friends. The reception follows, a sober, but lively gathering, designed by those in attendance to prevent the bereaved from being bereaved. Guests go home. Caterers leave. The sun sets, darkness descends, and a deafening silence settles over the survivors. Each goes to an inner place of solitude and pain. Exile.

The next day, well-meaning friends living out of town and offspring leave to resume their lives. To the one left behind is left alone, mourning, longing. More exile.

* * *

For John, life became a quagmire through which he dragged himself one leg at a time.

Work, escape from the pain, called a distant but audible voice inside his mind. *Do something, John, even if it is just getting to the office and sitting at your desk.*

His success seemed far away and not connected to the reality surrounding him.

Success had been exiled.

Every new day took him a bit further away from those awful moments. The awfulness began to lift. He thought about the call telling him of the accident claiming Mimi's life. Anger surged then subsided. Anger, that so capricious an act, the violent thoughtless and selfish disregard of another that took her at the zenith of her life. Anger that he was powerless over the consequences of what was to befall another man. Then he began to think about what he had had; what they had had, and peace returned. How they traveled from the beginning of life together to that fateful morning made his head spin. They had tried everything and everything didn't work; at the end of their respective ropes they simply gave up, and the pieces picked themselves up, and a new relationship was formed.

What joy, what contentment, what magnificent dust-ups and even greater makeups filled their days. They rode the crest of the wave as the waves dashed over them.

Throughout this mourning, a time of intense personal grief, a time when solitude was coveted, well meaning and those meaning well had been plying him with things to eat. Mimi had warned him of such a happening; they had laughed about it then, but now he grew cautious, curious. At first he ignored the doorbell and waited for the dog to get quiet, before peering out to see what had been the cause of the disturbance. On the doorstep, he found the first casserole with a note of condolence attached. More casseroles appeared. Some of the names on attached cards he recognized, some not, but he made every effort to solve the mystery and write a thank you note.

He was grateful for the ladies of the Casserole Brigade. What they brought, they had made. Casseroles were made by good friends, married, their concern genuine.

Several weeks later followed a series of casseroles presented in person, the givers no doubt emboldened by the passage of time.

Looking back, he laughed inwardly at the presentations of these culinary offerings, or were they culinary propositions? Each as different as the respective giver, and each giver as elegantly prepared as the bait they brought. One, as ebullient as a puppy scampering in the morning sun, and just as yappy, another dripping sincerity and concern and yet another just wanting to drop in and cook, right then, right there. Some wealthy, not so wealthy, open-and-closed minded, prudish, forward, dressed, semi-dressed, demure, brazen with one thing in common, lonely and empty.

"Just fine, just fine, you?" said with protruding lower jaw and the last "you" rhyming with "ewe". Sad sheep.

He recalled a fact he and Mimi had often discussed before she was killed. People who had an interior life attracted men and women of similar attitudes and outlooks. An interior life was an unknown to those who were unaware of an interior life. They were attracted by another's strong interior life made by those who had one that was attractive. The empty ones generally found each other and unknowingly perpetuated their misery. His experience told him that the empty were uncomfortable around those whom they admired; they had not much in common about which they could converse, other than news, weather and sports. They were the buyers of self-help books and flocked to hear the latest self-help gurus. The gurus were the beneficiaries of the empty.

At the door, John saw an envelope in the doorjamb. He didn't recognize the handwriting. Picking it up, he looked at it as if it might explode when he attempted to open it. The initials *ESP* were engraved on the paper. The note was simple, straight-forward: *Welcome home. Love, ESP.*

Who was ESP?

John tossed the letter onto a pile of mail. He quickly forgot about the strange note as his mind drifted to his wife's ghost who still haunted his heart.

The night drew them closer. Unaware of powerful forces working in their lives, sleep shielded them. Their journey conceived by unknown stirrings, neither felt the others presence. They had had their dreams and in dreams almost nothing works as the dreamer dreams.

Their deepest secrets and secret fantasies had not as yet been aroused from the centuries slumber. Genetic pass-through is like a tidal wave. It's always there, but needs a good shaking up before it gets moving. Once begun, it ends only as every shred of energy is spent, sometimes with disastrous results, sometimes swallowed in the vastness of the sea that gives life.

The innocence of sleep is blemished by the sleeper's subconscious bursting to the surface in perplexing parables. Wavelike, dream cycles either live or fade into the vastness of the unconscious.

Unaware they dreamed at the same time, they moved as one towards the inexorable intersection binding them. She thought of her final "yes" as a declaration, a beginning, a launching point into a new life adventure.

All that could be seen was seen through the eyes of a new and more glorious love. Past images and repugnant remembrances were forgotten. The panacea was fallible, as men usually are. Yes, she had known him. But that was at a time best forgotten except for the passion shared as they tried to make it work. Hollow orgasms signifying nothing deluded them at a time when delusion served them well. But reality rudely interrupted the union they had imagined. He was not, nor could he be, hers alone. The blinding possession of new love blinded her to his vocation, his life and passion. Wasn't she his passion?

He was passionate. Passion wrapped in several layers of smoldering intensity was a powerful aphrodisiac. Her body simply responded. Her mind was left to struggle with sensations exploding from every nerve. They had met innocently enough. They were strangers. Maybe the other's name had passed before them in conversation, but other than a pleasant sound, it meant nothing.

She watched him walk into the room. Her hair glistened in auburn strands entwined in a profusion of long waves moving in every direction, falling to her bare shoulders. Sitting on the edge of a chair, legs crossed, hands finely proportioned and long fingers excited him. He noticed her shoes were off, and his eyes were drawn to the almost too perfect feet with finely sculpted toes gently touching the carpet.

When she turned around, he saw blue eyes and a heavenly smile. She had not yet noticed him, which freed him to be a casual observer of her delicate person. Sleep deepened. Her body began to float deeper and deeper.

She felt her head on the pillows and moved her legs against the soft sheets as her arms flowed to her side, stretching sleep from her mind. She turned over, folded her body into a more comfortable position and urged her mind to recapture the dream. She felt her body skip beneath the surface of consciousness like a smooth stone bounding across a stream before it disappears beneath the water. Then she saw him through the ethers of a dream.

John went upstairs to his office, pulling his chair and himself in front of his computer. He began to write. A page then another; lots of pages scrolled down his monitor. Pages of anger pouring out of him, as he exhausted his rage and began to feel better. Looking at what he had written, an overwhelming sadness swept through him. He knew as Mimi looked from wherever she might be, she shook her head in disapproval of his actions over the past weeks. He was amazed that he could have been so vulnerable; she wasn't. He thought of himself as level headed, responsible, perceptive and aware; she knew his resources had been depleted.

"Why didn't you do something?" He spoke to her, hoping she would hear him; maybe she did, maybe not, but at that moment his eyes filled with tears and he sobbed. They were not tears of desperation, frustration, but tears of deep mourning, missing her. He did not try to stop crying.

He blew his nose, washed his face. He felt depleted, exhausted, empty and alone. He wanted to walk into their bedroom and find her napping. The bed was made, the shutters open, and the sunlight, almost too hot, was held at bay by the whooshing of the air conditioning. He headed into the bathroom and splashed what passed for cold water on his face. Looking in the mirror, bloodshot eyes stared back at him. His nose was red and running, his hair was rumpled and his shirt was damp and crumpled. He began to unbutton his shirt and found himself looking at his reflection in the bathroom mirror. *Need to work on that body.* He went to write.

His radio began to play music. "Time to get in shape, old boy."

Mimi's parents were thrilled to have John as a son-in-law. John's parents were more grateful for Mimi. John was an only child and having him home safe in one piece from the war was all they could have hoped. Too, they hoped for grandchildren. Mimi's parents were relieved that she had found the man she had dreamed about. That she had dreamed about a certain type of man was certain. John's mother and father had been good friends in college. By the time they graduated they had become engaged. Their connection, stretched by WWII, was never broken. Theirs had been a good, loving, creative, exciting marriage.

John inherited his father's strong work ethic, and from his mother an insatiable curiosity for most things in life found in and out of books. She had his grandmother's elegant bearing and looks.

His mother had an artist's eye for perspective that he inherited. His mother failed to tell him how much she loved him. That was cultural. It stung him deeply.

The Bensons, Margaret and Frank, cherished their son, John. John's parents had been steeped in the culture of the Victorian Era. Their ancestors lived a comfortable life in England for generations before their great grand parents immigrated to America. Margaret and Frank reared their son as their parents and grandparents had been raised. That was paramount in their lack of outward displays of affection for their only child. His father worked hard and successfully, as that generation did, and his mother raised her son. Margaret kept John on a tight rein, afraid she would lose him to some imaginary foe. She never satisfactorily explained her imagined fear to John when he finally asked.

John did what most all children are supposed to do: Grow up, move away, get married and begin a life of their own.

John met Mimi in college. After graduation John's journalism major landed him a good job with a national magazine. He found himself living in Chicago. His eye for perspective made him a very good photographer.

Mimi, an English major, earned a Masters degree in Education and taught English at a private school in Chicago. No coincidence.

They married, had a daughter and worked hard to insure a successful marriage and provide a strong foundation for their daughter Grace. They were married for over thirty years.

His mother once said, "The good die young." She never said they got killed walking with a friend. The speeding car missed her friend. Mimi was killed. In seconds she was gone. Gone.

When John Benson walked alone, he became aware of nature surrounding him. Spring was getting a toehold; flowers had begun to bloom. New bulbs bubbled into a profusion of multicolored azaleas, tulips and daffodils. Tender green leaves sprouted from branches as the trees shook off winter's hold.

He noticed people. More people were out walking and he was grateful that beautiful young women and beautiful older women were wearing less, as they walked along in warm spring weather. Their colorful costumes added to the colors nature generously provided. Not long ago the fall colors had fallen and the dingy gray of winter lent a pall to the city. Now much to his delight the colors magically reappeared in a brilliant bouquet. He slowed to admire the variegated tulips and azaleas and noticed a clutch of young women walking, talking and laughing as they passed by. With their multicolored hair, they competed with nature's palate.

Tender buds looked fragile, and as one of the girls brushed by, a new bloom it fell to the ground. Farther on, a newly hatched bird lay dead beneath its nest. Life continued, how fragile these things, baby birds, human lives. At once he was aware of what surrounded him and of the lives of those he loved and respected.

His inner vision became more acute as he absorbed the beauty and death surrounding him. The fragility of life, including his own, became real.

The home that they had shared was waiting for him. Warmth welcomed him as he opened the front door. He wanted to call her name, tell her the insight he had just been given. No

Mimi, but he knew if she had been there she would smile at his telling and would have touched his arm in silent acceptance.

The fragility of life was compounded as he missed her with every fiber of his being. Tears began to fill his eyes as he surrendered to the loneliness deep within. In his mind he resumed his walk through the grieving process. Without reserve letting go absolutely, the tears flowed. Time passed and he slowly composed himself. Sitting in her favorite chair, he watched moving images of their life pass before him.

The shrill ring of the telephone shattered his meditation. He let it ring two or three times and answered it.

"Daddy, it's Grace. You OK?"

Silence. He took a deep breath, preparing for whatever might be coming.

"Daddy, can you hear me? Are you OK?"

"Yes, dear, I'm here."

"What have you been doing today?"

"Grace, it's time for a new chapter to begin."

"What are you talking about? You are writing again?"

"No."

"Then what are you talking about?"

"Spring."

"Spring?"

Grace had a complex soul. She was pragmatic and romantic; the consilience made her alluring to men. She was tall, had long, thick blonde hair and brown eyes. Her eyes were wide set, which gave her a look of wonderment even when she was out of sorts. A beautiful mouth which could pout seductively, smile radiantly, and express any number of emotions, whether she felt them or not. She kept those she didn't trust constantly off balance and those she liked perpetually happy. Loyalty was valued, and she valued those who were loyal. Loyalty, not just to her friends but also to passions in which she, they believed. She was blessed with elegantly long legs, a beautiful face and a figure to compliment the first two.

She wanted to be a photojournalist like her father, but finance and Wall Street held her interest. She graduated from college with a degree in Finance and minors in History and Journalism. After graduation she got on with a medium-sized newspaper covering business news. In the two years she did this several awards came her way, but she soon realized that writing about business and the workings within the companies she covered might be more profitable if, instead of writing about them, she would buy and sell them. She applied for and got a job in the research department of a regional brokerage house. One thing led to another and she ended up in the Corporate Finance department of a major Wall Street firm.

The money she earned permitted her to enjoy her independence. Money was nice, successful men were attracted to successful women, but she soon discovered the kind of men to whom she was attracted were intimidated by women of her presence, integrity and success. To succeed she had to become tough—tough enough to not back down in the face of tough negotiations carried on by very tough, competent negotiators. Men who measured their success by the bodies left in the street, and the size, not only of their checking accounts, but their many houses, cars, planes, expensive schools for their children, jewels for their wives, and young mistresses, old mistresses occupying unlisted condos in faraway places. Their egos had one mission; her mission was to beat them at their own game, and she did. She was all business in her business world. Away from her work she enjoyed her own life with her own good friends. Grace had dated a couple of men on "the Street", but she found attempting to love their egos left her empty; she left them.

She met Jack in a bar. It was a small bar in the mountains in the West, and she was there with friends who shared her interest in finding out-of-the-way places. The town they were in had once been an active silver mining town. It nestled in a canyon along a major highway, and it showed signs of having seen better days. There were two churches, three bars, a gas station with a café attached, a post office, sheriff's office and a couple of other small businesses. The town was on the way to someplace, provided one was headed east or west. It had its claims to fame, but a little known claim being Robert Louis Stevenson's wife had lived there for five years after the Civil War with her Confederate husband, who was trying to strike it rich in the silver mines. He and the silver mines played out.

For Grace, Jack was put in play.

There they were. Not much to do in a place where there is not much to do except talk, or drink. They began to talk, and talk and talk, and they were still talking the next morning when the café opened for breakfast. They learned they fit. They fit each other. Her determination, intellect, toughness, beauty, poise, and serenity enthralled him. He, her Jack, was a man unafraid to risk life and limb for his passions, and she correctly intuited that he was passionate about his work, his life, and his friends. She found the adventurer and the romantic who was happiest absorbing the simple, quiet beauty he found in the mountains, and the carnage of war, a powerful, forceful, insatiable contradiction she did not want to live without.

They were both introverts masquerading as extroverts. There were many shared traits, both beguiling and unbearable, but those intermingled for the good to those who are in love.

Jack was a photojournalist. His career was jump-started by his involvement in the early days of the fighting in Afghanistan. He had read innumerable accounts of the Russian invasion and of the resistance to the Russian invasion. His sense of adventure had taken him there in late 2000, and he had decided to stay in Kabul, using it as a base from which to explore and meet whoever would meet with him. After 9-11 and after the U.S. bombing started, he was able, because of the people he knew, to position himself to photograph stunning portraits of mayhem and pathos.

Jack was a few years older than Grace, four maybe five, but his experience made him seem mature beyond his years. Aside from her obvious beauty, he was attracted by her inattention to her physical being. Yes, she took care to look good, but beneath the surface was a woman he wanted to know, and in knowing he fell in love.

Part Two

Three Women

Chapter Four

John sat in the seat next to the aisle with his left arm around the empty seat beside him. He observed himself sitting and wondered whose shoulder his arm would someday caress. The preacher was launching into one of his history lessons, so John let his mind wander. He knew whom it was his arm would not caress. A voice whispered, "You were ripe for the plucking."

Jack's inner voice spoke:

Snared, yeah, I was the one who thought I was being so cool. I was thinking I had dealt with my wife's death. Six months was it? No maybe seven, but regardless I guess I was just fooling myself. Someone said it would take a year. I guess I just wanted the pain to go away, and Gail conveniently appeared, and she appeared to be the answer I thought I was looking for.

Finally the preacher began to focus his remarks on *the Old Testament* lesson. *Why don't they ever focus on the Song of Solomon?* John wondered.

The gray clouds made the cold day even colder. He shuddered against the damp chill as he left the service. He decided to take the long way home. The car radio was off and he began to think more about Gail. John was tall, if a couple of inches over six feet was tall; he liked tall women between 5'7"-5'10" and Gail fell into the middle ground of tall. He liked her blonde hair and hazel eyes. She had soft, almost too thin lips, lizard lips. Her presence in his life was made easier for him because she, although divorced, came from that element of society known as "socially acceptable". It became effortless to find the peer approval he deemed necessary to justify his jumping into the world of beyond-middle-aged dating. He looked at one's life span as 120 years, and that was how he saw himself, middle-aged.

About the time Gail loomed on the horizon, John was beginning to feel a bit better about his lot in life. Throughout, his old friends had stayed in touch. His wife's friends were sporadic in their communication for the simple reason that married women really are not comfortable with the perception that being alone in a house with a single man would create. Her single friends respected his wanting to be left alone with the exception of the Casserole Brigade.

That Gail had had multiple previous husbands raised a few eyebrows. It was difficult to determine who had left whom, but in any event their partings seemed amicable. There was a son from the second failed union, and failure at being a parent would one day haunt the parents. Gail was absent from her son's life, as was the boy's father.

Gail was successful. An attorney, she had married an attorney, who was the child's father. Now divorced, she was enjoying her career as well as her single status. She was available, but guarded her privacy. Her success and her demeanor intimidated some men, turned others off, and the ones who hung around she simply discarded. Gail prided herself on her looks and firm body. Her goal in regularly working out had less to do with how well she felt than how well she looked for a woman more than midway through her forties.

Her son was the product of two people who loved themselves and their work more than their child. Able to afford nannies, Gail dumped the child with the nanny whenever it was inconvenient to have him around, which was most of the time. The result was predictable. Trouble became the boy's constant companion. Unable to get attention and affection through the normal channels, he set about with great success to wrest whatever he could get from whomever was willing to play along. Whether the price was in dollars, or emotional currency, it was an expensive exercise. Gail found that the nature of her relationship with her son was repellent to the men in whom she was interested.

She had known someone who knew John was an easy entrée, and a party was arranged. That someone Gail new was Evie Patterson. Gail thought it a simple plan to throw herself at someone who was stumbling in a cloud of grief. Someone who would, in his vulnerability, be more than happy to have a woman of her stature and looks shower him with attention and sex.

John was invited to Gail's party, and told that an attractive, successful single woman would be present. He found himself looking forward to a change of pace, meeting new people, new women. Much to his relief, the party was to be a small group of friends, both of his and the host's. Small was good. He asked a friend about the mysterious single woman and learned her name, occupation and status. She was blonde as best as one could tell, hazel eyes, good figure, nice smile, liked the out-of-doors, maybe too socially ambitious, liked to travel, practiced law. Her ex was a named partner in a large law firm, had not remarried, a man who kept a low profile.

Another woman was there who had not originally been

included. She was an acquaintance of Gail's who had worked with her on a high-profile case, which with Evie's help, Gail prevailed. Evie Patterson had a small but successful public relations company specializing in the medical instrument business. The companies manufactured specially designed orthopedic devices used in the replacement of joints, knuckles, hips, knees, shoulders and elbows. There were devices for open reductions, aiding in getting bones to grow together, or lengthen limbs, or inserted into broken bones. One company specialized in exotic metals and compounds successfully used in repairing fractures sustained by football players, allowing them to return more quickly to their team. It was this company that Gail, with Evie's assistance, had successfully defended. The majority shareholder and his wife who were giving the party were also Evie's friends.

Evie operated below most peoples' radars. She was an astute observer of people. She was intuitive and had a sense of humor that allowed her to observe the interaction of people without people knowing they were being observed. The more egregious their behavior, the more overt their actions, the more obvious their motives, the more she enjoyed it. Having spent time with Gail, all in a courtroom, she respected Gail's ability. Maybe the cool professionalism could be tempered in social situations, maybe she could be more feminine, more soft and sexy. She had the body, but Evie wondered if Gail had the humility to pull it off.

Evie knew how she felt about John. Evie was attracted to John. She kept this secret from Gail. Evie's brief introduction to John at a party given by a friend of John's two months prior to Gail's event had been a pleasant surprise for Evie. At least that's what she had gleaned by the way John stole glances at her. She sensed that his initial attraction towards her had been mutual. Unfortunately for Evie, John completely forgot the evening.

John arrived suitably late, which was against form, as he was usually to the minute for all parties as he was for assignments. This gave him time to scout the room, not that scouting a dozen people was complicated. He spotted Gail before she noticed him. She wore a suitably short skirt, silk blouse, suitably snug, top two buttons open. She wore stylish shoes with medium heels. Her makeup was in place but didn't overwhelm her pretty face. Blonde hair fell softly around her face and graced her shoulders. He made mental notes and went to get a drink.

"You must be John," a woman said, the Scotch arriving at the same time she reached the bar.

Turning slowly and taking a half step back, he took her in, smiled and said, "You are Gail." He held out his hand. She looked at the hand and her conditioned reflex to shake an outstretched hand found her taking his hand. His hand took hers, gently, firmly. His long tapered fingers reached around the back of her hand, and she looked into the eyes looking at her. They were not smiling eyes; they were not soft. They looked at her, not into her eyes. They just looked.

Gail was lost in the quandary of wanting to pull free and wanting to gently close her hands around his. Those eyes, they really saw what they saw and she felt x-rayed. She looked back into John's eyes and they smiled, briefly; the smile gave her a start.

From across the room, Evie watched. Evie smiled.

Chapter Five

At the church, John sat in his usual seat; left arm around an unseen companion. Anticipating the lesson. The upbeat songs of praise and adulation were sung with the refrain being repeated three times, maybe more. There had been times listening to the pastor that John felt himself walk through hidden spiritual doors. He knew the preacher was right about people living with their dark side, not knowing or admitting if they even knew they had a dark side. His faith, both practiced and taught, told him the only good thing about him was what his Risen Lord had given him.

For too many years John had labored under the delusion he was good, and if he did good things, to be doing good things, he'd be better. Not true. He had the interior scars to prove how not true the old ideas had proven themselves. What he really valued in the preacher was a man who spoke the unvarnished truth, and to him that truth was like cool, clear water. He knew in his soul the rocky years of his marriage were his own doing and that any rough patch was his responsibility. "To the husband goes the blame, to the wife all the glory." Hard words, true words, words John knew he needed to hear and act upon. Words he had not heard nor acted upon when he was married.

The statement that "people marry illusions, and once the illusion is exposed what is left is what one really married" was the real reality. It flowed both ways. He wished he heard those words when Mimi was alive.

Their marriage flourished. The illusions they had had been shattered. They learned to live with the reality of who they were. Their marriage grew; their love grew; their friendship and passion grew. Her death was not an illusion; the grief was not an illusion.

His brain did not want to believe what was obviously apparent to his friends: Gail was selfish, self-absorbed, manipulative, and at the moment a sexual predator. His acknowledged weakness was for women who had a sultry, practiced sexuality. They walked a certain way, looked the way they walked and dressed for success of a different sort. They were successful, and the combination of success and sultry was his aphrodisiac.

The following week in the church, he watched himself sit with his arm around his invisible partner. The singing was heading into the refrain for the umpteenth time, and the preacher was facing his flock, arms upraised as he swayed to the music. The night before John had been with Gail and driving home, he heard Marty Robbins sing "Devil Woman Let Me Go". Somehow Devil Woman seemed to fit his mood more than the Blood of the Lamb.

"People live in dark side without even knowing they are there," said the preacher. "It's easier to live in the flesh than in the Spirit. Those who criticize the licentious become the legalists who wrongly assume they are pure. They are just as much a part of the dark side as those they deride."

John knew it would be a long hour. Right now it was easier and infinitely more fun to enjoy, savor and marinate in the delicious memories and scents of Gail's dark side.

Gail went out of her way to service his every need, and he found he had needs he didn't know about. The feelings of violent ecstasy were followed by waves of nausea, as the reality of her perverted purpose infected his feelings about himself and for her.

Gail took John to clubs where people went to see and be seen, to meet and be met, and openly flaunt their latest catches. Blissfully unaware of her motives in taking him to these places, he found them fascinating and was mesmerized by the rituals of the other patrons. Seemingly oblivious to her manipulations, he was seduced by the sexual adventures, the primal activity and lastly the exquisite pleasure he experienced. He had the fever. Her occasional and deliberate flirtations with younger patrons stirred him to more demonstrative efforts to hold her attention in these surroundings. He was in her environment, playing by her rules. The Evil One smiled on her.

John woke, got ready, and headed off to the small room serving as the preacher's "church". This time Marty Robbins' Devil Woman didn't play. What John heard and what the man said had been two different things. He heard the Dark Side explained as anything that took one away from God's will, or was it His intended purpose? Intended purpose? God's will, whatever that was, was not what he'd been doing.

The delusion that participation in anything remotely clandestine and "out there" has no ripples, camouflages the reality that the night really does have eyes. No one knows who's watching, or listening. His mind jumped to the verse in a prayer he said after receiving the Eucharist in his mother church: "... so to assist us with thy Grace ... Whose property is always to have mercy." There had been any number of times he and Gail had evoked the Father's name during the zenith of carnal mindlessness, but he didn't think that Grace had anything to do with that.

His good friends seemed more than interested in his new situation. John did not tell tales, but his friends' wives had an underground network that would have made the CIA jealous. Word of John's goings and comings as well as Gail's designs were surprisingly accurate. Jerry Adamson had known John in both good times and bad, and they had a deep, long, honest friendship. Jerry's wife, Joan, had been a close friend of his late wife, Mimi, and their daughters had grown up together. Libby, their daughter, was close to Grace.

"Jerry, have you heard anything from or about John lately?" Joan inquired one evening about six weeks into the affair.

"No. Should I have?"

"Don't you know Mark?"

"Mark? Oh, you mean Gail's ex? No, but I know someone who knows him reasonably well, another attorney at a different firm. Why are you asking?"

"Just heard some things."

Jerry raised an eyebrow at his wife. "What sort of things? Oh come on, John has better instincts. What are you really saying?"

"I haven't said anything, yet."

"What have you heard and from whom?"

"This is going to take longer than a commercial; can you

spare the time?"

"Spare me."

"I had lunch with Libby last week, and she mentioned that a friend of hers who sometimes moves with the "in crowd" had seen an older couple at one of the places she goes. Seems they put on quite a show for the younger set. The funny thing was, according to Lib's friend, was that they thought they would not be noticed, you know, groping, kissing, going a bit too far. Next day Lib's friend was with some other people who had seen the scene, and she began to ask around and found out who it was. It was Gail and John."

Jerry and Joan gave each other a funny look.

She continued with her story, "Well, a couple of days later I was with Sue and Beverly, and Sue mentioned what Libby told me. When I asked what it was all about, Sue said other friends heard similar stories. Beverly said she had a friend who knew Gail through a paralegal in the same firm, and she said she heard Gail was using John as some sort of passport to respectability. And she's got that delinquent son hidden in Europe. Every descent man she's been with has dumped her because of that baggage. Seems as if no one credits Mark for trying to do something with the boy, but Gail bought the boy off in so many ways. What it boils down to is that I am worried that John has lost his mind and is about to or could do something he'll regret for the rest of his life. Any chance you will be seeing him soon?"

Jerry shook his head. "No, but if it will help, I will."

Chapter Six

People who observe without being observed know a great deal. Evie Patterson was not a part of any crowd. She listened. She knew there was nothing she could do regarding Gail's plans, nor did she wish to interfere with the natural course of events. She had an idea what the result would be and how Gail and John would play out. She knew from experience a relationship rocketing from the front door to the bedroom door sowed the seeds of its own destruction.

Spring had become summer and the heat was warming John throughout while he walked. As he walked he began to reflect upon the past weeks. There had been his lunch with Jerry, a worried call from Grace questioning his sanity, and his coming to grips that his friends had begun to act as if he might be contagious. He walked listening to his footfall. A car passed, slowed and toot-tooted its horn. He looked as Gail's car moved down the street; he turned right, heading up a hill. He listened to his footfall.

On Sunday Gail manufactured another creative excuse not to go with him to hear the pastor. As he sat with his arm around the empty chair, he sensed it would not be Gail whose shoulder he would one day caress. The song of praise resonated around him and the knowledge he must end the affair settled in, but carnal euphoria tamped the rational feelings to nothingness. William Blake wrote that the Devil resided within man and the ensuing conflict between good and evil was infinite. Remembering that, John had the strange feeling he might be sleeping with the Enemy.

He heard the pastor speaking about the inner presence of God. "It is within, only within, where you will find the Creator's presence. It is strength, conviction, purpose, and truth and the power to achieve to originate, create. It is not by your power but the power of the One within, the Holy Spirit, that one perseveres against evil. Whatever you have outside yourselves that you believe empowers, elevates, enhances or otherwise gives your life real meaning, permanent meaning, is Evil's doing. Evil never sleeps."

John felt the preacher's eyes boring into his.

Later, John walked into his home to the ringing of his

phone.

"How was it?" Gail's voice was on the line.

"Church, just fine. I'm going for a walk."

"Walk? I made reservations at the Club and asked Susan and Carl. They're going to meet us at one o'clock."

"I'll get there when I can."

"What do you mean 'when I can'? I've made an effort to do this; besides, I really want you to meet Carl and Susan."

"I'll see you there."

"Why are you being such a shit about meeting some friends of mine?"

"I'll see you there." Hanging up, he went to change.

The doorman held the car door open. Gail got out. She turned to see Susan and Carl walking towards her.

"Hi, good to see you," she chirped.

"Gail, you look gorgeous, as always."

"Carl, you're a married man!"

"Married to me, thank God," Susan laughed.

Susan looked behind Gail, "Where's John?"

"Oh, he got home late from that church he goes to and wanted to change. He'll be along. Let's go in. A drink would taste good."

* * *

John walked in the opposite direction. Maybe there might be something he hadn't noticed by walking the usual way. He hoped for new ideas, insights, answers to what troubled him, and at that moment what troubled him was having her second drink. His mind working backwards from the present to their first moment together and then back to the present brought the reality he sought.

The pastor's words settled with a thud into John's consciousness: "You are in God's heart. Don't worry whether or not He's in yours. If you have trouble believing it, just say it until you believe it: 'I'm in God's heart.'"

John tried when he first heard it, and remarkable things happened, and as he walked along he began to recite his old mantra: *I am in God's heart and in His mind.* He walked and let the heat of the day embrace his body.

The summer heat deprived the grass of the women looking for the right shade of tan, walking their dogs, riding their bikes; it was quiet. Sweat began to drench his shirt and streak his shorts; he breathed harder; his pace quickened; the answer slammed into his mind.

What he hoped above all else was for the serenity to act firmly, without rancor, but with sufficient force of mind and emotion to accomplish what he knew he had to do.

He took a cool shower and decided to let the cold water drench his hot body until he felt himself begin to cool down. Taking a cold shower in the summer was not easy as the cold water was almost warm. It took awhile. He dressed carefully and headed off to "The Club" to meet Gail and her friends.

The doorman greeted him with a smile, and John could smell the aroma of grilled roast as he walked in the door. The room was large but the booths and tables were arranged to respect privacy, and several semi-private nooks overlooked a manicured garden above a creek whose banks were shrouded in ivy-covered bushes. Gail, Susan and Carl, seated in one of the nooks, were engrossed in an animated discussion and were unaware of his approach.

Gail's voice reached him as he drew near.

"He really pissed me off this morning. I mean, he just blew me off like I was a moth, and no one, nobody treats me that way and gets away with it."

"Gail," Susan cautioned, "why don't you just calm down. I agree you were treated badly, but cool it before he gets here."

"Ha, that weak excuse of a man hasn't the stomach to show up after the way he spoke to me."

"Don't underestimate John Benson. He's not the limp dick you think he is."

"Carl, just who or what is this prize I'm trying to capture before the Little Bastard comes home?"

"What 'little bastard', Gail?"

"J… John, you look great. I'm so happy you got here before we ordered."

"What little bastard, Gail?"

"Drink? A Martini should taste good after your walk."

"No. No drink. No food. No more you."

"What do you mean by that?"

"We are through."

"What are you talking about? Are you on something?"

"I had lunch with Mark last week. You're familiar with Mark?"

"Why didn't you tell me? You Bastard, you kept it a secret?"

"No secret, just waiting for the right time to tell you. Now seems like the right time."

"What did he tell you? Lies I bet."

"No, no lies. He was very forthright about your relationship and how you both dealt with Cody. Cody, remember your son coming home from Europe next week?"

Carl coughed, interrupting them. "I think you two might want to be alone at a time like this. Best we get on our way, right Susan?"

"Carl, sit." John placed his hand on Carl's shoulder. Carl sat.

John then said, "Gail, I really owe myself an apology for being such a fool believing you as I did. But I don't owe you anything but contempt for the way you deceived me. All you wanted from me was my soul. There are qualities about you that are easy to love, but they're covered beneath layers of selfishness, anger and resentment. The good stays buried. Goodbye."

John turned, walked out and went home.

Chapter Seven

His house welcomed him. He turned to close the door and saw an envelope on the floor. It was engraved in dark green ink with the initials *ESP.* Opening it, it read, *It's a new day, Love Evie.*

The note seemed odd, especially after he had just broken up with Gail. Now he had a secret admirer? And who was Evie?

He listened to his voice messages and read emails. He had a message from a magazine editor asking him to call; Grace trying to get hold of him with some "really big" news, and Jerry left a short message to call him back. There was also a message from Evie Patterson wanting him to call. He wracked his brain to place Evie Patterson. Whoever she was, he decided he wasn't interested in meeting anyone new right now and deleted her message.

Two days later he had been reading the paper at breakfast, when the doorbell rang. He opened the front door and saw a striking young woman standing on his doorstep. "May I help you?" he asked.

"You are John Benson, are you not?" Her voice sounded familiar, but he couldn't place the face.

He looked at her, taking her in.

The young woman stood smiling. She had captivating eyes—big green Audrey Hepburn like eyes—and dark auburn hair pulled back in front, falling to her shoulders. Her ears were delicate and perfectly shaped, adorned with small, golden earrings with emerald stones that matched her eyes. Her alabaster skin, her full lips, her smile—an Eva Gardner smile.

Her eyes looked directly into his, and he stood transfixed, wondering how a siren such as this could suddenly appear at his door. "Do I know you?"

"My name is Evie Patterson. We met once at a party. I heard that you had recently ended things with Gail and . . ." Evie's long tapered fingers held up a foil-covered plate. I brought you a sweet potato pie to lift your spirits."

After fending off so many women showing up at his doorstep with seductive dishes, John kept his guard up. "Miss Patterson, why did you leave me the two notes I found on the floor of my front entry? The timing of your last note was impeccable. Were you hiding somewhere in the Club's dining room, watching me break up with Gail?"

"What are you saying? I most certainly didn't spy on you. Maybe I kept tabs through friends who happened to be in the right places at the right times. When Gail took you to those clubs to be shown around like her prized show pig, I knew your relationship was doomed. Oh, the note . . . it was just good timing and good luck, I'm hoping." She smiled. "May I come in?"

"Well, I can never say no to sweet potato pie." He stood aside and motioned her in. He then reached for the plate she carried. Their hands brushed briefly and he felt the smoothness and warmth of her skin. "Thank you, Miss . . . May I call you Evie?"

"Yes, please do."

John led her into the kitchen and pulled out some plates and poured two cups of coffee, while Evie cut them each a slice of pie. They retreated to his table on the back patio overlooking the garden. As they made small talk about the lovely weather and how the flowers were in bloom, John took delight in the pie's sweet taste and looking into Evie's sparkling green eyes. She was so pretty and so young. At least half his age, he imagined, if not more.

When she finished her pie, she started to blush. "John, I must confess. I was thrilled to get the news of your breakup. Knowing that Gail was finally out of the picture and the playing field had been leveled was manna from heaven."

John felt a surge of excitement that a beautiful young woman would be attracted to a middle-aged man who was well past his prime. Perhaps dating a gorgeous socialite such as Gail had made him more appealing to women of all ages. Or maybe Evie was just another gold digger hoping to latch on to a wealthy widower. He could never be too sure these days.

Not ready to show his cards just yet, John only nodded at her confession. He was definitely intrigued by her and began to ask probing questions to see just what kind of woman he was dealing with.

He quickly discovered that Evie Patterson had led an interesting life. She looked younger than her almost forty years, a lot younger. Her youthful face had been both a blessing and a curse. In college she was looked upon as an oddity. Blessed with brains, looks and practical ability, her classmates joked about her being a "child prodigy". She majored in philosophy, the history of ideas, and literature. She had the gift of languages and spoke several. Her native language was Hebrew. French and German came next followed by Arabic and Farsi.

"Why Arabic?" John asked her.

"When I looked at what was happening in the world, I asked myself what two languages would be most important for me to learn, Chinese or Arabic? I chose Arabic and Farsi because I am Jewish. I attended primary and secondary school in Israel. For college I had scholarship offers from all the big name schools. I chose Hobart because it was and is one of the very top liberal arts colleges in the Unites States.

"Hobart and William Smith Colleges are located in Geneva, New York. They trace their origins to Geneva Academy, established in 1797. The history of the school seduced me, as did the region."

John was impressed by Evie's intelligence and passion. She was definitely a woman who went after what she wanted. She captivated him as she described her family history. Her grandparents had immigrated to Israel from the United States in the 1950s. Their ancestors, three generations back, left the Pale Settlement for the Unites States at the end of the Nineteenth Century. Catherine the Great established the Pale Settlement in 1791. The Pale was where European Jews living in Russia were sent, many in chains. Catherine did not want "the Heathen Jews" doing business with Russians. The Jews were not allowed education and were treated as outcasts. They were confined to an area known as the Pale.

The Pale was bordered by modern-day Poland, Latvia,

Lithuania, Ukraine and Belorussia.

Between 1890 and 1914, approximately two million Jews immigrated from the Pale to America. Regardless of a new life in America, Evie's ancestors clung to the old traditions. In the early 1950s, Evie's parents immigrated to Israel. They longed to find the community they had as children. They worked as educators in public schools in New York State. They knew of the anti-communist sentiment sweeping the U.S. They did not support communism but their heritage, Russian Jews, made them targets of abuse. Having saved enough money to leave the United States, they made the necessary preparations and moves to Israel settling in Umm al-Fahm, located 47 miles South Southeast of Haifa.

Culturally, Evie stepped out of the traditional model. She attended schools in Umm al-Fahm from first year through eighth and secondary boarding school in Haifa. She excelled both academically and socially. Her beauty and sex appeal made it easy for her to choose rather than be chosen. This attribute did not go unnoticed.

The Mossad had kept an eye on Evie's family since they arrived in Israel from the United States in the 1950s. The atmosphere in the United States was then colored by Senator Eugene McCarthy's anti-communist witch-hunt. The Mossad wanted to be sure Evie's family had no communist sympathies. Doing that, they by accident stumbled upon Evie.

She was in secondary school at the time, and in no way resembled the awkward schoolgirl the Mossad first noticed. The Israeli Defense Force kept its eyes open for men and women who fit a certain template. Agents observed Evie, noting how she controlled the groups she associated with. She was the lead actress in theater in secondary school, as well as a top field hockey player. Academically she was at the top of her class. Her choice of colleges, Hobart Sarah Lawrence ranked high in the eyes of her observers, and they noted with delight her interest in the languages of the surrounding area. Because of all Evie was, and because of her charisma, the Mossad approached her at the end of her junior year of college, when she returned to Israel for summer vacation.

Evie was sanguine about the opportunity, and danger, this new opportunity presented. It also presented the opportunity for advanced language and cultural studies at a Mossad training facility. This would happen after she graduated. All this she shared with her parents. They were supportive of their daughter. They were supporters of the State of Israel and quickly validated her future plans.

Her training began at the beginning. The physical hardships dealt out to all new trainees by the IDF were strenuous. The goal of the trainers was to push the mental acuity of each trainee to the maximum. Evie, they pushed the hardest. The additional training for Mossad operatives emphasized mental toughness even more. She grew stronger, more beautiful. They put her in the field, operating within Iranian borders. Her assignments differed, utilizing every skill she had been taught.

When Jerry Adamson alerted his superiors about the photographer who was his client, Evie went to the United States and took up her role as an expert witness. She was trained to understand more about orthopedic replacements than the engineers who developed them. That was how she became acquainted with Gail.

"Wow," John said. "I had no idea you and I ran in the same circle. And all this time you had been keeping tabs on me and Gail?"

"I never thought she was right for you. You deserve a woman who will treat you much better." Evie gave him a look that he interpreted as an invitation to make his move.

John felt the heat rising in his body. Physically, Evie had all the qualities he desired in a woman. Her intelligence and straight-forward approach was refreshing. And her vibrant youth made him feel young again. But because of their differences in ages, they could never be anything more than just lovers. For once, following his pastor's advice to walk the high road, John did not ask Evie for her phone number. She looked disappointed as she left his house, and a part of him regretted not exploring what this intriguing woman had to offer. But having just ended his turbulent affair with Gail, John had no intention of jumping from the frying pan into the fire.

Chapter Eight

That afternoon the phone rang. It was Grace immediately inundating John with statements and questions. He said, "Whoa, slow down, breathe, one thing at a time."

"Daddy, didn't you get my message? Why are you so hard to reach? What happened, where were you yesterday? Great news at work, much better news about Jack. We have absolutely wonderful news!"

"What's the wonderful news?" He wanted to get her talking, about anything, and he knew talking about Jack would take her away from her opening line.

"Jack proposed yesterday and he got down on one knee and had this wonderful ring, that even fit, and I'm just . . . we're just so happy and . . ."

John felt the tears. Happy tears flowed, happy that he could be happy for and with his daughter; honest happy tears spilled out of his eyes and ran down his cheeks.

"Daddy, Daddy, are you there?"

"Yes."

"Well?"

"Well what?"

"Well, you know, don't you know, are you listening?"

"Yes, I'm listening, so is your mother wherever she is. I was thinking about how really happy, excited she'd be to hear this news. Have you set a date?"

"I miss her so very much. Well, it's August, and Jack and I were thinking about late April or early May of next year. That gives us time to plan. Daddy, we need to be together to plan effectively."

"What the hell does that mean? Who is this 'we'?"

"Oh for God's sake, who did you think I meant by 'we?'"

"We, Jack and Grace living under the same roof, you know, moving in together, same bathroom. Getting to see who gets the cold seat in the morning, you know."

"You're going to live in sin, officially? Are you telling me that you and Jack are already getting used to close-quarter drills? Give me a break!"

"No! We are definitely not living together, yet. Spending long weekends together, maybe toothbrush here, there, everywhere, but my 'delicates' stay in my drawers, no pun intended. And as for Jack, he can be more of a prude than you."

"Prude, me a prude?"

"Yes, you. Got to go. I love you, Daddy."

"Love you too. Tell Jack how happy I am for both of you."

John felt a lump in his throat. He remembered how he and Mimi would talk after dinner, speculating about the man Grace might marry. They even guessed one young man was "the one", but they guessed wrong. As it turned out they never would have guessed correctly.

The next morning as he was having coffee and reading the paper, the phone rang. John looked at the Caller ID, picked it up.

"Jerry, what's on your mind?"

"What's on yours is what's on mine. You've been busy."

"Busy? Other than a call from Grace telling me she's engaged to Jack, it's just a normal Monday morning."

"Congratulations, the best kind of news. We need to have a chat."

"About what?"

"Gail."

"What about Gail? Ended yesterday. You know how pyrotechnic relationships flame up and out."

"John, don't try to duck out of this. I've known you too long and we know too much about each other's lives. Ended? You threw me a hard, high curve this time. What happened?"

"To tell the truth, I don't know what happened, exactly, but if you have time and want to come over for a drink I'll attempt an explanation."

"Sure, John, what time works for you?"

"Five-thirty?"

"See you then."

That afternoon, Jerry drove up and let himself in.

"Good to see you, Jerry, you know where the whiskey is. Whiskey makes my job as host and the one coming clean a lot easier."

"Want one?"

"Not now, thanks."

John was glad his friend had stuck his nose into his mess. He was comfortable exposing his underbelly to Jerry; he knew his old friend would not abuse the privilege.

When Jerry took a seat, John said, "Are you set? This might take awhile."

John had used his time walking, both this day and the past

months since Mimi's death to try to plumb the depths of his emotions. What emerged was a mosaic of his life, as he understood it. He found pieces of his childhood—early school years, boarding school, college, girlfriends, first and only wife, his business career and the men and women who mentored him. All of these had embedded themselves in his persona, but the biggest piece of the mosaic was the one person he wanted the most but who gave the least. His mother's influence was enormous and finally he stopped trying to analyze it; it just was. Out of this composite slowly emerged a man who had risen to the top of his profession.

Along the way he picked up a camera and that became an instrument of his excellence. What he couldn't frame with the camera, words met the occasion. He began to attract notice from the top weekly magazines and well-known periodicals for his photography and his writing. His writing looked deep into the core of the people and places he wrote about, and photographs illuminated depth and feeling, whether bird or beauty. His media expressed his deepest feelings.

"Jerry, how do I manage to screw up the simplest things like my life or what's left of it? Where or how do I start this sordid tale?

"After the funeral everyone seemed to flee like rats on a sinking ship. I pretty much kept to myself. Mimi's friends and some friends of her friends brought casseroles until I thought I would go nuts, so I quit answering the door. Then one day this gorgeous, almost-redhead came by and just walked in and announced that she was so and so. Now, she had great flare, looks, sparkling eyes, smile, and that mysterious something. I was not interested in finding out just what that something was. I deferred; she left. I wish I could remember her name. Anyway, time rolled on. I decided that I had better get a grip and explore the world once again, so I went out a time or two with women who just wanted to go out, nothing intimate, just a movie and supper. There were no expectations on my part and no pressure."

"You mean you actually acted like a gentleman?"

"I *was* a gentleman, thank you very much. Jerry you know that preacher I talk about? Well, he said something awhile back, and I went home to Mimi and practiced what he said he did, and our marriage flourished. Mimi didn't really understand what was going on, but in time, without saying anything else, something changed in both of us. I became more of a husband and she more of a wife.

"Care to share the secret?"

"Pastor Jim said to tell Mimi that my role in our marriage was not to make her happy. My responsibility was to treat her as the single woman God chose for me to marry. I am to treat her with love, respect and dignity."

"That is a real paradigm shift."

"Works."

"I guess what happened between us happened between Mother and I before she died. We allowed each other to be who we really were. We loved each other as mother and son, and gave each other the room to love and be loved.

"Going out was a big deal. If Grace had not pushed and prodded me to get back out there, I'd still be holed up. Under the present circumstances that looks pretty good. But off I went and each date became more and more comfortable, and being more relaxed about the whole love dance I began to let nature dictate. I liked the attention and the pleasure. Then I went to a party, and there was Gail coming on to me. Do you know what it's like having a sexy woman come on to you? I thought I was so cool, a real magnet. And Gail played me for all it was worth. I played back and it got crazy wild out of control. It was as if all I attempted to put into action with Mimi was erased the minute Gail slid up to me. I was defenseless."

"John, what turned the tide?"

"A couple of things opened my eyes. One was Grace questioning my state of mind, and the other was something the preacher said. He was going on about the dark side. The fact that people call themselves Christians doesn't make one a Christian. I think he used the word "saved" to describe the effect. My opinion, and that's all it is, is that some people who declare themselves saved are rotten, miserable people. Next time you run into one, look into their eyes. You're liable to see little zest for life, just a dull bulb. They think their exempt from the affects of their former behavior, so they just keep on doing things as they did before. Looking for people to blame, never looking at the truth about themselves, and quick to "praise God", pray for something not bothering to look at them. They are hiding behind the Bible, because it's convenient to use 'the Word' as a shield against the realities of their lives. They also use 'the Word' as a cudgel to defend indefensible positions.

"I once knew a man like that. Used to think he was really a good person who valued loyalty, but I was wrong. Not his fault? No, mine for being so gullible. Saved? Not a word I trust until I see whomever walking the walk, and I've seen them and they are real. Anyway, the dark side is where we all live. Just made a broad generalization, but if the seven deadly sins and a host of others are not the dark side, well, I'm wrong. The dark side is a familiar place; lived there most all my life."

Jerry sat forward. "Explain."

"There is a period in my life I don't talk about. Oh, Mimi knew; there was nothing about me she didn't know, and things I didn't know until she told me. She was good at pointing out my defects. And that was fodder for the fire of my anger. I don't know too many people who appreciate having their defects paraded before them like yesterdays laundry. Anyway, that dark period was when I was overseas covering any battle I could. And sometimes I was able to manufacture a few battles, which is really easy to do. I liked the life on the edge. The men and women on the fringe have a lot to offer. They live in a reality of survival, hustle and divided loyalties. They are loyal to themselves and make no bones about it. They use people with impunity and manipulate with such a practiced ease the mark hasn't a clue. They are inventive and creative. They survive by their wits and guile, and when necessary, brute force. I lived that way for about a year. I hope you realize I'm describing every person walking around out there. Hell, if we could see behind closed doors it'd be a horror show. Even in the so-called 'best' neighborhoods and schools the dark side is the only side. Why do you think people walk around screwing up their lips and giving it the nasally 'just fine, just fine.'"

Jerry's face was now cringed with judgment. "John, why are you so angry?"

"Because it makes me mad as hell to do the very thing I detest in other people. I got into the game and it turned out to be a dirty game. And what makes me angrier is my ignorance of what I was doing. Leaping into bed became the most important event of the day or night, and everything before and after was just a means to the end. Gail's not to blame; *I am,* and not being able to point the finger of blame makes it tawdry as hell. I detest people who live a lie to get, without regard, what they covet, and I lived a lie to get laid—well laid."

"Well, you screwed up, my friend. You extracted yourself before it really got ugly, and did so without creating a huge scene. You got lucky. I'd like to say you took the sophisticated route but what's done is done. Look, get over it and quit driving yourself crazy. Yes, you were vulnerable, yes, your ego and the little guy ran away with you, but in a few days you'll feel better. Why don't you go see Grace and Jack? Sitting around here mourning Mimi and nursing your embarrassment helps not one soul, especially yours. Leave tomorrow."

"I should have looked at Gail's hands and shoes instead of something else."

"What's that all about?"

"A long time ago my father said you can tell a great deal about a person if you look at the person's hands and feet." In business, whenever John met a male client for the first time, he always observed their hands and feet. Fingernails that were neat and trimmed and shoes that were shined meant a man took pride in what he did. Granted some men who looked sharp but whose motives were corrupt usually had something out of sorts with their hands, shoes and what they wore. The look they wore told most of the tale, but hands and feet were the biggest "tells".

Men who had broad stubby hands tended to work with their hands. They wore scuffed boots or hiking shoes. Men who had narrow slender hands and fingers were more intellectual. Artists' hands were not delicate. They were sculpted. Shaking hands with either group, John could pretty much determine whom he would encounter. A woman's hands and feet had just as many tells.

"And . . . ?" Jerry asked.

"And, had I looked at her hands and feet, instead of something else, none of this might have happened."

When John felt he had confessed all, he walked Jerry to the door and shook his hand. "I'm going to go see Grace and Jack. Call you when I get back."

Chapter Nine

The plane lifted into the air. John fell asleep.

He slowly woke up and felt eyes fixed on him. It was an uncomfortable feeling, having alien eyes sweep over his face, coming to rest on his eyes. Turning toward the direction from which he sensed the alien presence, his eyes slowly opened. Fully open, he was looking into green eyes that sparkled with a strange familiarity. His eyes moved up to find amber waves of hair shining in the light streaming through the plane's window, then down to full lips pulled into a brilliant smile and down to a smooth neck and down and down. "Are you stalking me?"

"No."

"What are you doing here? Serendipity maybe, coincident maybe, curiosity, good planning on your part, maybe you bribed the ticket agent?"

"No."

"Then what?"

"You won't believe me, and aside from that you probably don't remember my name, so why should I even think about justifying myself to you?"

"Evie Patterson, what the hell are you trying to tell me?"

"You do remember my name! John, go back to sleep. I like watching you breathe."

Standing in the baggage claim in New York, he looked for his suitcase, and as he saw it make its way onto the carousel, an arm slipped into his and he looked to find Evie, bag, coat, tote, and a big smile. The bag slowly slid by as he looked into her eyes and, nodding his head up and down, agreed to take her to her hotel.

He called Grace on his way into town. Yes, he had planned to arrive on the late side and didn't or couldn't meet Grace and Jack until dinner the next evening. He had planned a hot shower, good sleep, quiet morning, and the afternoon just wandering around New York. Plans change.

Men are not very smart. Those words had come from the

pastor as he had launched, for the umpteenth time, into another sermon about marriage, its problems, solutions and illusions. From what John heard and remembered there had been some good advice, and in a humorous way, that pushed buttons deep within his maleness that didn't like or appreciate what was being said. Now, too late, too whatever, he rolled over and found himself next to a very naked woman sleeping with a smile on her lips.

There she was. No makeup. She was beautiful. Her closed eyes danced in front of his, as if dreaming. Smooth, full lips, contoured cheekbones, wonderful nose, sculpted chin, soft, no blemishes of any kind. Her body was firm, full, and malleable. Even her feet and toes seemed perfect.

There he was. His face had the worn look of someone exposed to harsh climates, and the crow's feet at the edge of his eyes and almost-sagging skin under his chin stood in too sharp contrast to the young woman next to him. Hell, he was walking around on replacement parts. But, he remembered another woman he knew, an attractive woman, had complimented his good looks, and murmured something under her breath about him being sexy.

His vanity was short lived. He got out of bed and headed into the bathroom. Looking in the mirror he recoiled in horror at the face staring back, stubble, tousled hair, sagging pecks, butt, and waist. Shit!

He looked around for his toothbrush, razor and the mini apothecary he carried on trips. All he could find were Evie's makeup, birth control pills, hairbrush and blow dryer. Undaunted, he stepped into the shower and began soaping off. Water streaming over his head, he felt something soft press into his back, as two hands reached for his stomach. One hand pulled him close; the other reached farther down and began to gently massage him. He didn't move. The water beat on his head. His stomach tightened beneath the touch of her hand. He could feel her nipples hard against his back. He turned and her mouth pressed against his, and her tongue slipped between his lips and found his tongue. Her leg rose against his side, wrapping around his waist. He moved slightly against her as her hand guided him into her. Leaning back, he braced himself as she began her assault on his body. They erupted together, and he felt himself sliding slowly to the shower floor; her body draped around his.

The water ran over them.

Room service arrived with food and coffee. Wrapped in a towel, Evie answered the door to her hotel room. John looked across what served as a table and wondered just how he had managed to find himself with a woman, younger by who knew how many years, acting as if he were a middle-aged stud or a not-so-young *roué*.

"Evie, how did we end up here?"

"You offered to bring me to my hotel, remember?"

"Yes."

"Well, I invited you in for a drink, and since you pack light, you and your bag ended up being taken to the room with mine."

"And?"

"And we went into the bar for a drink. Well, you do remember the music, the dance floor, and dancing with me, do you not? And do you remember we had more than two drinks?"

"And less than how many?"

"Less than four. You asked me to dance, and you are a really good dancer, and the music slowed down, and you pulled me close."

"You mean you tried to get into my clothes."

"Something like that." She laughed. "Anyway, one thing led to another, and as I moved against you, I could tell you were interested in more than dancing; so, I kissed you and you kissed me back, and then I became interested in really getting into your clothes."

"Yes, I remember, but who led whom where?"

"You led me to the elevator. You kissed me in the elevator, and somehow my skirt kind of got close to my waist, and then before it stopped, your belt got unbuckled. On the way to my room I found myself being carried, except I helped out by wrapping my legs around your waist and then your shirt came off. Don't know how the door got opened, but by the time it was closed we were, well, we were . . ."

What is it about men, or a particular man, that after a certain age younger women have the ability to hypnotize, seduce, render almost useless the strongest of men? A fling might be one thing but an older man pretending to be a younger man is an unreasonable spectacle regardless of how respectable one might imagine one's self. It's an alchemist's addiction. One can't turn lead into gold, and a younger woman can't turn back an older man's calendar or Mother Nature's, regardless of how much a man desires.

Evie said, "I find you so irresistible, I wanted to . . . ?"

"To what? You wanted to seduce me?"

"For starters. I've been attracted to you for some time now. Back when I met you at the party where you were introduced to Gail, I became intrigued by you. I almost approached you then, but Gail swooped in. She was practically salivating all over you. I worked with Gail, knew her type, knew you were vulnerable. I was curious to see how that all would work out. I became a spectator. And it was fun to watch. I really thought she'd set the hook pretty deep. But you threw it and threw her out of your life. She was furious." Evie gently stroked his arm. "Remember when I came to your house? Were you not intrigued, a bit interested?"

"Curious. Taken back a bit, yes intrigued, but I wasn't in the place to pursue anything with anyone at that time."

"And how about now?" she probed.

They were interrupted by the ringing of his phone.

It was Grace calling.

"Father, where the hell are you? Who is the woman? What's going on?"

"Whoa, slow down, and remember who you are speaking to."

"Yes, sir. But when I heard you had danced off in the arms of a really good-looking woman, I . . ."

"Who told you I danced anywhere with anyone?"

"Well, you're not exactly an unknown commodity, are you?"

"Meaning?"

"One of the people I work with happened to be in the hotel lounge when you were there last night and recognized you. I have your picture at my office. She saw your performance and thought it might be of interest to me. And it is of great interest."

"Oh."

"All you can say is 'Oh'? I thought you came to see us, Grace and Jack, just the three of us. And now you've got this *woman* hanging all over you."

"Grace, relax. I am here to see you and Jack. We're meeting for dinner. I'm coming to your apartment for a drink beforehand. I'm coming alone."

"Ok, but all this comes as a shock. You just got rid of that disaster Gail and now you're acting like a man on the loose. Don't you have any sense of proportion? I heard Mother say that to you one time she was furious with you, and I feel the same."

"Grace, feel any way you want. There is one thing I'm not going to do and that is get into a skirmish on the phone. We can discuss all this when I see you. I'll come earlier."

"How much earlier?"

"An hour, maybe. Bye."

He put the phone down and breathed deeply, doing his best not to show the hurt he felt.

He looked around, found his suit coat draped over a chair, pants on the floor, shirt by the bedroom door. No wonder the waiter smiled when he brought breakfast.

Evie came over and began massaging John's shoulders. Her hands felt good; she found knots, worked them out and kissed his cheek. He turned and looked into those wide, soft, comforting green eyes. What passed between them was more than words could express.

"What do I do now?" He got up, took her in his arms, and held her tightly to his body.

She yielded to his arms, and as her body folded into his, her breathing became deeper, louder. The intensity of his feelings aroused her, moved her, took her, and she began to move slowly against him. He felt her legs against his. She could feel the hair on his thighs, and her thighs moved slowly against, around and in between his. She felt him come alive. Her robe slipped off her shoulders, and her full breasts and hard nipples pressed against his chest. She stood on her toes to kiss him and felt his hand move over her bottom and his thick, strong fingers massage her and she gasped. She lifted her leg to absorb the waves of ecstasy moving up and down her body. She heard his breath, felt his chest heave, and his hands lifted her off the floor and gently laid her on the bed. She clung to him, was a part of him, and as he came into her there was a burst of light and her head spun and her body convulsed deliciously against his. She felt his arousal and responded as never before, clinging legs locked tight as his body rocked against hers. She felt his hands move under her and lift her to him as he moved more quickly, more urgently, moving and moving and moving deeper as his passion exploded into her. Her back arched and bucked; her breath caught in her throat; he gasped and lunged, and she held him and he held her. There was silence.

He showered alone. The water streaming hot and hard massaged his body, and the soap lathered and worked into his pores. The water hit him and washed away the soap in streams running off his legs and feet.

He watched the water, flowing eddies whirling down, gurgling down, spiraling down the holes in the drain. He felt like the water rushing down, rushing and rushing. He used his hands to scrape the water off his body, grabbed a towel and began to dry his hair. He felt a towel rubbing his back, turned and kissed Evie gently on the lips, those full, soft lips. "My turn." She smiled at him.

"See you later tonight."

"If you're lucky." She blew him a kiss.

Chapter Ten

It was later than he wanted it to be. He headed towards the museum. He bought a ticket and headed to the Old Masters. It would be quiet, he hoped. Quiet, quiet, quiet enough for him to sort through the happenings of the last hours. He found a bench where it was quiet and began to sort out just what he had done. His choices, actions, behavior, and feelings he'd never had. Ah, yes, feelings that rose to greet him from some alien part of his brain. Feelings Evie aroused in him.

"Aroused." He chuckled as he thought about that word. An older man, a young woman, the arouser of a woman, what? Evie was thirty-something years younger? Just what had he gotten himself into?

He left the museum with more questions than he had answers. He caught a cab and rode it across town. The cab pulled in front of Grace's apartment building. He got out and walked to the front door. He was greeted at the door not by Grace, but by a doorman. The elevator was not too rapid, not too old. The ride to the 20th floor gave him a bit of time to utter a prayer. He finished as the car slowed as it came to a stop.

The door opened and there she was, running to greet him. They embraced and he felt a tear against his cheek. He gently took her arms and moved her away to get a better look. Her large brown eyes gazed into his and a wisp of blonde hair fell across her brow.

He gently, as fathers do, moved the hair off her face. How he loved his daughter. That love directed him to let her lead the conversation they were about to have. She'd hand over the reins when she was ready.

She led him into a not large, but very comfortable living room/den. There were two bedrooms, two full baths, modern fixtures, and a decent-sized and well-equipped kitchen with granite countertops in green and alabaster colors lending warmth to the whole apartment. She had decorated the living room with some of his photographs, as well as paintings by young New York artists she had begun to collect.

There were brass lamps with tasseled shades. The sofa's fabric blended with lamps, some of the paintings, and set the room off as the one lived in the most. They had old leather chairs that she and Jack had nursed to a bright luster with what she thought was too-expensive leather balm. There were bookcases filled with books and odds and ends she had gathered while living there. It was warm, sophisticated, welcoming.

He sat in one of the leather chairs and she perched on the arm. She crossed her beautiful legs. Her dress was not long, nor too short. John thought she looked radiant, spectacular. Success had not spoiled her, and her natural, real interest in other people was evident. The subject, he saw it rising to the surface. He took a deep breath and braced himself.

"Daddy, what is going on with you? No sooner do you get rid of *That Woman* than you end up in a hotel with a woman I didn't know existed . . . and you tell me to 'relax'!? This is supposed to be a big time in my life, and here's good old Dad acting like I don't know what. No, I'm not going to relax until you can explain to my satisfaction and maybe yours just what the hell is going on. Jack's due here in just under an hour. I suggest you get started."

"Well, you certainly take after your mother, don't you? The 'That Woman' disaster? Well I, well, fell into a well-planned ambush, and for a brief period she let me think I was leading the dance. But Gail's plans crashed, and I was able, with help from Jerry, to move on. He told me to get on a plane, get away, to come see you, celebrate with you and Jack. Current events stretch even my vivid imagination, so sit back, relax, and don't jump to any conclusions."

So he began from the beginning, leaving nothing out of the timeline. When he finished, he probably had more questions than Grace, but, from the look in her eyes, Grace's questions had less to do with Evie than with her father. Grace had patience and good sense beyond her years. Regardless of how many different ways she could question her father's rationale, she let an inner resource guide her to say nothing. Well, almost nothing.

"You have got to be kidding me."

"No."

"What are you going to do?"

"I'm not sure. But..."

The buzzer buzzed, announcing Jack's arrival. Grace went to open the door, but before she got to the door John asked, "Care to meet this mystery woman?"

"Yes, when?"

"Tomorrow, brunch, say ten-thirty at the Carlyle. Please include Jack."

"Pretty uptown. This will be fun."

Jack greeted Grace and John. They had a couple of drinks

and moved on to dinner. The conversation revolved around their plans, their hopes and dreams. John took it all in and thought how familiar it all sounded. His mind drifted back to similar conversations with Mimi when they were newly engaged. His mood softened, he joined the conversation and reminisced about his experiences at the same time in life. He did not lecture. Life would be a far better lecturer. Nothing was pinned down as far as a wedding date or where it might be held, but that was of little import as the festive, loving mood promised a resolve.

Outside the restaurant, they said their goodnights, got into cabs, and went their separate ways.

He slid the door card through the slot and wondered what would greet him. Would she be there or be off with some of her friends who lived in the city. The door opened to dimmed lights and a soft voice welcoming him.

"Have fun?" she asked. "I've been thinking..."

Before she could finish he interrupted, "So have I, and have some serious questions to ask."

"Such as?"

"Why did you lie about your age?"

Evie looked offended. "What are you talking about? You started this age crap this morning, remember? What makes you question my ability?"

"I'm not questioning your ability, just your age. Someone in their early thirties is not going to be hired by the likes of Gail to bail her ass out of a world class jam, right?"

"Well, perhaps, but I am quite curious, well-educated, look younger than I am, and besides, I found the solution to her problem." Evie glared at him. "Your reputation precedes you, my dearest man, and when I found you on the plane, well, I just, you know, thought if I could maybe seduce you, not really bed you, intellectually seduce you, thought it might be fun. I had no idea the brain, body and heart would collude to conspire against me."

"That's nice, but doesn't answer an important question—how old are you?"

"Truth?"

"That would be preferable."

"Well, let me look at my fingers and toes for a moment, and we'll see what that produces. Good thing you're here to help me count. Let's see . . . twenty times ten plus five . . . looks like thirty-five. Yep, that's it, good ole thirty-five. Are you happy about that? Had you believing you'd be arrested for statutory rape or something, or embarrass the hell out of yourself for having a child for a lover, didn't I?"

She threw a pillow at him. "Don't you know when a woman has fallen for you? I mean fallen hard. Get over yourself. What kind of insult are you throwing out to me? Good grief, you think a few more years would make me more respectable, less of an embarrassment; that I'll be more acceptable to be seen with you in public with your daughter? Get a grip, big boy. You are a man who has spent one night with a younger woman. One night giving all to that woman, who, by the way, has given all of herself in return. Do you think I make it a practice of seducing men in the shower? Do you think I'm the type to make love around the coffee table? If that's what you think, or feel, see you later."

At this point in a lovers' quarrel, the man can choose to respond in a number of ways. The best, most humbling way the preacher had preached is to accept one's fault, admit wrongdoing, and stand before the prosecutor, awaiting whatever judgment might be handed down. Furthermore, admitting one was wrong, offering no excuse, pointing no finger, no whining, no pandering, nothing, can be disarming. He stood, eyes fixed on hers.

"It was your body," he blurted out. "Yoga? Pilates?"

Silence.

"Evie." A statement not a question.

"Yes." She was expecting a fight. She feared a fight. She was afraid of reacting too strongly, of pushing him out of her life. She could taste the fear in her mouth. Anger and rage waiting their turn.

"Evie, I was wrong." Words from the past ran through his mind.

"And?"

"And, I was wrong to have questioned your motives, questioned your age, questioning anything that has happened between us. I was wrong, period."

Tears began to run down her cheek. Her lips quivered as she drew back the covers and walked slowly towards him.

"You're wrong? No excuses, not even a whimpering excuse, no copping a plea? I want a good-screaming, clothes-throwing fight, and all you can say is that 'you're wrong'? Come on, John, tell me a tale. Tell me something so absurd it'll make me laugh until I really start sobbing."

He stood. Her eyes expressed shock, fear, rage, and malevolence. John Benson was transfixed by what he'd just absorbed.

Evie spoke, "It was the kiss."

"What kiss?"

"The soft, lingering kiss this morning sang to me of love, bliss, excitement, contentment. My imagination fired. John, I am well aware involvement with an older man can be a double-edged sword. Old friendships could go away, or Grace might detest the idea of her father being with a woman who is close to her age. I was wrong. Your age has nothing to do with anything. My age is the problem. Life can be cruel."

"Evie, would you like to meet my daughter and her fiancé? Breakfast at the Carlyle, eight-thirty?"

Evie stood, still not wanting to move. Silence speaks volumes. She had not planned to fall in love. She did not want to fall in love. She did not need to fall in love. She was a hunter, not a farmer. The excitement for her was the chase. The chase was over, had been over and there she stood, captured in a trap of her own making.

"I love you. Oh, how I love you. Yes, I want to meet your daughter when we go to the Carlyle."

Chapter Eleven

When John returned home from New York, Evie sent an email saying she'd be staying in New York through the weekend and the following Monday, and be home Tuesday. She wanted him to meet her plane. And to please call her even if the answer was no.

Jerry called John, reminding him of their meeting. He told John his assignment was out of the country, if he wanted it. He'd have to leave in about ten days and would be gone six, eight weeks, maybe longer.

Grace wanted to know that he got home in one piece, and there was a message from a woman he'd never met wanting an interview. She said her name was Lilly James. She had a throaty purr to her voice and left a phone number, and, yes, she would call back if he didn't call her.

Yes, he'd meet her and take her to dinner. That would be good. He returned Jerry's call to get the particulars on the new assignment. It involved a long trip to the Mideast. Jerry told John that he was offered well above his usual fee for this assignment.

The phone was deep in her shoulder bag. Evie began the extortions one sees when a woman wrestles with a large shoulder bag or crowded pocketbook as a cell phone begins its melody. She pulled it out, flipped it open and breathlessly answered the call. Her spirits jumped as she heard John's voice. Stopping in the entrance to a shop selling high-end shoes, Evie caught her breath and, yes, she could hear him clearly.

John began with words of endearment, words from his heart. He worked his way around to telling her that their time together after her return home would be cut short by an assignment he had committed to take. This was not something Evie anticipated. She was angry. Upset, she wanted him intensely. At the same time not caring if she ever saw him again. She started to say something mean, caught herself. She decided to cry. She choked back tears, whimpered. She heard nothing, silence. She hung up.

John closed his phone. It rang, and rang, and then stopped.

Evie never heard him say he would meet her plane.

Evie's flight was on time. He drove up to the curb outside baggage claim as she came out. He was out of the car and hurried to greet her. She knew about his assignment. She wanted to be angry about his leaving so soon, but when she saw him her breath caught in her throat. She let go of the suitcase and hurried to his arms. She smelled his smell, kissed him and pressed herself close. He pulled back, looked down at her and kissed her again. Grabbing the suitcase, he swung it into the back seat. She sat cross-legged in the front. Off they went. They stopped in front of John's house.

Reunions seem sweeter when the fruit is freshest. Theirs was no exception. They didn't smoke, but perhaps in the time it might have taken to smoke a cigarette their thoughts turned to time. The two months they would be apart seemed an eternity.

Later that night as they were sitting in bed, he asked if she knew a woman by the name of Lilly James. Her answer was both a statement of fact and a question that hung in the air. No, she didn't know Lilly James, but who was she and why did he have to know who she was?

Uncertainty about a phantom rival made her tense with jealously. Evie wanted to take him prisoner. No assignment, no being gone two-plus months, and hell no, no Lilly James, whoever she was.

John relaxed and sank back into the mattress. He watched Evie as she reacted to his query. There had been no intent to arouse suspicion or even the minutest question of another woman coming into his life, let alone a woman named "Lilly". He watched Evie as she wrestled with the conflicting emotions flowing through her veins. He watched. He learned. He put his arms around her and gently, softly kissed her. His leaving lost its threat. Lilly James became just another name.

Morning of the first day, he drove her to her home and she extracted a promise he promised to keep. Yes, he would take her to her favorite, but not fancy, restaurant for dinner. He carried her bag inside her house, kissed her goodbye and went about his business.

He called Lilly James. The woman had a throaty drawl, a smoky texture that gave the impression of someone who had a story. He was curious. He liked the way she wrapped her words in a shroud of experience, sophistication and sexiness. She wanted to meet him, interview him for a story. Find out about his life. When, she asked, could they meet? Drinks, dinner, afternoon delight—she had a sense of humor. He said he was busy for the next couple of days but later in the week would work. How long, where did she wish to meet? Would there be anyone with her? They settled on a Starbucks they both knew. She said he'd recognize her by her long, thick, dark blonde hair. What about the rest of the outfit? He was told not to hold his breath. He hung up and turned his attention to packing his gear.

Evening of the first day, the sun was setting. He arrived at Evie's, and as he ascended the walk, the door opened. He stopped. She was alive, beautiful beyond words, eyes flashing. He caught his breath and continued to walk slowly towards her. The lights of the house illuminated her in a way he would never have imagined. It was as if she were draped in one very porous piece of cheesecloth, nothing, or very little of nothing was left to his imagination. The night of the first day rolled into the morning of the second.

Friday arrived. John arrived at the Starbucks, looked around not seeing anyone fitting Lilly's description. He sat down at a table with a good vantage point. He waited. Then he noticed a woman walking towards the door. She wore a long, although not-to-her-ankles long, paisley skirt, with a slit in the front that managed to show off a reasonable amount of attractive leg, as she walked with a purpose. She knew how to make an entrance. Making an entrance without being obvious is an art form coming from tutelage and practice. She was well tutored.

He rose and pulled out a chair. She smiled and sat crossing her legs. She gave a warm welcome. He asked what she would like to have. He brought her tea. He had coffee and they looked at each other in silence.

Lilly blinked, took a deep breath and asked him how his packing was coming.

"Fine," he said.

"Good," she replied.

John took a deep breath and asked her why she wanted to speak to him about his work. She moved to the side, repositioning herself in the chair without regard for the behavior of her skirt. He looked; she smiled. They made eye contact. She began to ask him about his career, the death of his wife, his grief, his life, and about his new assignment.

"You want my life story?"

"Please."

"There's not enough time."

"Installments?"

"How many?"

"That's up to you."

How much did she know? Why was this important in the first place? John thought of himself as the dullest subject he could imagine. That was contrary to popular opinion. He decided he might as well set straight any errant facts, if she had any. He doubted she called him on an ill-informed whim. He suggested she begin with what she thought she already knew. She did. She did so with insight and clarity, and as he listened, he listened to someone who knew a great deal about him. He got up; she stopped. She got up.

. Lilly looked at him and asked, "What, or about what are you passionate, really passionate?"

"Let's walk around a bit, and I'll do my best to answer that question. Why'd you ask?"

"Most everyone is passionate about something regardless if it's big or small, animal, vegetable or mineral. From what I've read, you've had your share of passion. I count your late wife and a certain young woman."

"What certain young woman?"

"Don't be coy with me. I've been around, and things, situations, people like your young woman do not go unnoticed, at least not by me."

"Well, you've touched on a few of what you call 'passions'. But you overestimate my abilities and emotions. By the way, are you jealous?"

"Of what?"

"My young woman?"

"Why on earth would you ask me that?"

"I'm looking at an attractive woman, what mid, late forties? You come in draped, sort of, except you like showing off your legs, and from watching I'd guess you take good care of yourself, right? Don't seem to wear any rings, at least not anything suggesting an attachment, or one of those rings women wear when they're not engaged, but want to slow down any advances. You are asking personal questions of me, so I decided to ask some of you."

"Not entangled in a relationship, at the moment. Doesn't mean I'm celibate. Doesn't mean I'm not interested, or my radar's turned off."

John gave her a look.

They walked along in silence. Lilly broke the silence. "Might we get together after you get back from wherever it is you are going?"

He said, yes, that would work. She watched him walk to his car. He got in and drove off. He glanced in the mirror. She was watching. He smiled. Lilly's question about passions played in his mind, and knew she was spot on about two of his passions. He thought of the coming evening with "his young woman".

He drove home. Getting out of the car he watched a butterfly flutter away from a rose bush. He watched as it flapped along, the currents moving it first one way and then another before it settled on another flower. He went inside, stretched out on the couch thinking about the butterfly. It seemed determined to go from one flower to the other regardless of what the breeze did to its line of flight. What, if anything, did that have to do with passion? Its survival and the reproduction of some plants depended on that butterfly getting around, or was that bees? Before the next passionate thought caromed through his mind he fell asleep.

Part Three
John Dreamed

Chapter Twelve

When John returned home from New York, Evie sent an email saying she'd be staying in New York through the weekend and the following Monday, and be home Tuesday. She wanted him to meet her plane. And to please call her even if the answer was no.

The galaxies sparkled in the reflected light of the long dead sun. She sat calmly staring into the frosty night as her planet, cooling in the early night of deep space, hurtled towards a known, yet unknown, destination. He took off his jacket as the morning heat from the new sun beat on the asteroid. He looked over the rocks into the distant darkness and his dream led him to a far, far away place. Their, his, her gaze, their dreams caressed out there, somewhere. She slept; he welcomed the day, such as a day was on an asteroid.

She dreamed of him. He dreamed of her. They met in their dreams.

The morning sun gently caressed her face, gently, slowly moved down her almost sleeping body, caressing all of her. Stretching, moon glow faded into day. Stardust fell from sleepy eyes opening slowly to be kissed gently by the light. Taut arms, stretching legs, arching hips anticipated . . . what? Awake, the day began again.

He dreamed of seeing her moving in gossamer gowns, flowing as the breeze billowed the folds into the rays of the sun backlighting her delicate, soft, beautiful body. Her breasts sculpted her chest, her stomach, flat and hard, swept onto shapely hips. Her hips shaped by Beauty flowed into perfectly proportioned legs. Large, expressive blue eyes gave her face depth; a delicately shaped nose. Full lips gave her a radiant, sultry, inviting smile. Blonde hair fell gently on perfectly-shaped ears, perfect ears. She was alive in his dream. Then her hair and eyes, her whole face morphed into the one he knew. The one he didn't know; the one for whom passion loomed passionately and tore at his heart. He felt his stomach ache with unbearable longing for the one he wanted, the one who had had him, the one whose passion he had yet to return.

She morphed again and he stared into Mimi's dead eyes.

Her mouth opened, her lips formed words he could not hear. Out flew Death touching his cheek with long, bony fingers motioning him to follow. She morphed once more and Lilly stood above him. Her long skirt with the slit was blown back, exposing a blackened, charred body with bloody stick legs. A cruel smirk twisted her full lips into a fearful mask of broken and rotted teeth. Death danced her dance, and as she danced she became seductively wanton. Her delicate hands reached to draw him to her heaving breasts and lunging thighs. Strong, loamy musk pulling him into her against his will.

Lilly vanquished death with passion. Her passion longed for him. He reached for her. His hand was empty. He moved to kiss her full on her moist mouth. Mist swallowed him as she vanished into a galaxy sharply lighting the reaches of dark space. He ran to catch her hand, and as he ran he moved backwards and grabbed the scaly hand of Death.

He shook the hand with all his worth and Death's hand detached. John ran harder, racing backwards. His legs ran harder, his stride lengthening with every step. He sped backwards. He slipped from his body and watched.

She came to him quietly, slipping her hand into his. He could feel the gentle, delicate touch. He felt the bony hand of Death pulling them both, John and Evie, into the darkness, cold, alone darkness.

Darkness only dreams can fathom entrapped him. He saw her in the light as darkness slowly consumed him.

"Passion, passion, passion!" she called to him, as she slowly became one with the light.

"Wait, wait, wait for me . . ." His lips formed the words but the words were swallowed, muffled by an invisible hand he could neither see nor feel. He felt himself floating, going nowhere.

Assignment complete, final payment made to his account, John boarded the plane, anticipating. Anticipating seeing a stranger? Eight weeks absent from the intensity of lovers' lust can cool the ardor of the most arduous. Not communicating, or hearing an adoring voice can make that once-adoring voice whisper, "Shit." It was dark when the plane's wheels squeaked as they began to spin on the concrete. At last he was home; home, hail the conquering hero; to the victor go the spoils.

He stretched his arms and legs as the plane taxied to the terminal ready to be greeted, by whom? He hoped she would have read the email and would be anxiously, longingly waiting to envelope him in her arms. He was one of the first passengers with luggage through Customs. He entered the elevator. The door closed in front of him. Then it opened and he stepped into a crowd of waiting relatives and friends. There were men holding name cards, parents looking anxiously for loved ones. People embraced in joyous reunion. Lovers pressed together in eager anticipation of what was to be. He walked forward, searching the faces, looking for her hair, her eyes, anything to know she might have been there to greet him.

His heart raced anxious beats of its own. Sitting in an empty chair, he checked the arrival time, the gate number over and over hoping he had gotten her the right information. Eight weeks was a long time.

Where he had been he could not let her know how much he missed her. When he could, he sent messages, left messages, checked for messages in return. Busy, she was busy he kept telling himself. He had been busy. Had been in in harm's way longer than he would have liked.

He had worked. Lost himself in the images soon to appear on his computer. He became his images. That was his separation point from other photographers, his ability to blend into the images before they became images. His passion was obvious to all; it was alien to him. It was so much a part of his being. The emanating passion framed his work. The images came alive. They had a soul, his soul.

He stepped into the night. He felt soulless. Loneliness descended with a force unknown to him. His feelings, his confidence, his being was rocked from the inside. He walked towards the cabstand with a heaviness he had not known. Mimi's death had moved him like this.

Man's ego is fragile, easily bruised, seldom crushed. His felt pulverized. His feet weighed unknown pounds as he dragged them along. He got into a sweetly smelling, smelling-like-bad-incense cab and hoped the driver understood his address. The trip seemed an eternity.

Lights greeted his arrival. Too many lights greeted him. He noticed the lights glinting off a chrome fender of someone's car that was pulled well forward in the drive. Paying the driver, tipping him well, he dragged his gear to the door and got out his key. The key turned freely in the lock. He tried the handle; it yielded to his touch. Cautiously he walked in the door. Suddenly he caught the scent of perfume; its odor was like an elixir giving him a jolt of anxious anticipation. Maybe, maybe he would find her. Could be he'd find Grace home for a weekend and she had bought new perfume, could be.

"Darling, is that you?" floated from a door he suddenly didn't see. Her voice, her voice out of the void brought hope. John suddenly experienced an emotion so new, so intense its foreignness held him in check. She swept through the door, standing before him. The mirage didn't fade away but moved toward him, sheer gown flowing behind, revealing a body he thought so perfect he couldn't touch it, fearing it would disappear. The body enveloped him. Her hands caressed his face, sliding behind his neck, pulling him down to warm wet lips hungrily seeking his. His hands slid slowly down her body and slowly drew up the hem of her gown, finding silky, warm, anxiously wanting flesh forming to his hands. Her hands began undoing whatever blocked the touch of his body being against hers. She pulled herself up and wrapped her legs hungrily around his almost naked waist. She watched as he ripped off what remained. She pulled him to her and let her body engulf his.

Untangling slowly, lazily, tenderly, his eyes still closed, a smoky, sultry voice rolled into his senses: "You kiss a camel before you came home? Darling, I believe the term for your condition is 'ripe', and you are ripe."

He wanted to do something. Thinking for a second, he knew that he had already done something so completely foreign it shook him to his core. Without a backward glance he got up, went into the bathroom, took a shower, brushed his teeth, and got into the bed. Not a word was spoken. Sleep.

Lilly watched with amused detachment. She knew he knew. How to construct a bridge of trust upon which they both could stand was of more immediate concern. It could wait until the sun came up, which it did. She watched him fall into an uncomfortable sleep. His breathing was labored; he turned from side to side and onto his back. He coughed a deep rattling dry cough. Lilly put her hand on his arm. John settled into a deeper, less disturbed, sleep.

Lilly woke. Judging from the light coming into the room, she got up; time for coffee. She put on a robe, went to the kitchen, brewed a pot of coffee and waited. Walking to the door, she looked outside. The morning paper was waiting. She retrieved it. Glancing at the front page, obituaries and sports section, she decided that today the world would hold together. As long as stories about ill-behaved movie people took precedence over wars and rumors of wars, there was little real news to report.

Coffee done, she filled two cups and headed to the bedroom. John was propped up on an arm, coughing a dry, painful cough. They smiled as he took the cup she offered. The coffee's aroma embraced his senses, and the warmth of the first sip fell gently into his stomach, warming him as it went down. Lilly sat next to him and silently sipped her coffee. She could feel his body heat. He did not move away; he did not move any closer. Their bodies began a dialogue, communicating warmth and closeness. Neediness, a foreign unpleasant sensation, crawled into the pit of her stomach, landing with a thud, vibrating through her body. She got up and went to the bathroom.

He heard the shower. He got up found his robe and shuffled

into the kitchen. His mind was on central time. His body was ten hours ahead. He poured another cup of coffee, sat down, grabbed the paper and tried to focus on what it presented. He heard Lilly walk up behind him. He turned and saw she was dressed, smiling as she headed to the coffee pot.

"John, I've never done anything like this in my entire life, not even imagined doing something like this."

"Well, I was hoping to have been met at the airport last night by someone else. I never expected to find you here. Certainly not the welcome I anticipated. What happened? Something happened to motivate you to find a way into my home. I mean, good grief, I morosely walk into my house, and there you are, practically naked, wildly seducing me. Before I knew what had happened, we were making love."

"I enjoyed it very much. To answer your question and to find a way to keep on doing what we did will be difficult to put into words. Over the span of eight weeks quite a bit can happen. Time, used wisely, is a wonderful collaborator. I told you when we first met that you were not flying under any radar, social or otherwise.

"John, you have a reputation. People clamor to see your work. When I first started researching, I didn't just find accomplishments, awards, wonderful moving photographs, I found a person. The man who became his subject, a man whose passion filled the frame with life, color and sensitivity. I've researched lots of people and could not find the depth or breadth of who they were. It became a dispassionate occupation. I could disconnect and find whatever I wanted and not feel a thing.

"Then you became an assignment, nothing more. I was going to dig around in your private and professional life, find everything worth finding. I had a job to do. I sifted through old interviews and articles. I found a strange attraction, a foreign sensation. You mentioned a couple of books that stirred your imagination, so I read them. As I said, time became a co-conspirator."

"You read those books? What did you find about me? They were stories that took me away from what I was doing. They were fantasy, pure escape."

"They were for me as well. I found a man who loves to play. We don't play enough. Life is hard. Life comes at us from every direction. Life assaults both sensibilities and senses. The playful man is a rare man, a man who does not run from his deepest feelings. Something or someone opens the playroom door and he's the first one through. How wonderful, how rare to have found that man."

"Don't put sticky notes on me just yet. Yes, I like to play. I once heard a priest talking about play at the altar. I had to think about that for a while, but in my days as a Chalice Bearer, I learned about play at the altar. It's an inside play. It is respectful of the Liturgy of the Eucharist. It's play emanating from within. It's a Gift. From that I learned the real meaning of playfulness."

Lilly nodded as if she agreed. "Having found you terribly interesting and attractive beyond words, I continued to snoop around with the purpose of disproving such a man existed. I had never come across anyone like you. I've had relationships; they came and they went. They went because they take themselves so seriously, and my transparency scares them away.

"John, I found out from your peers and some of your friends that what has happened since your wife died happened because your anchor in life has been yanked away. You were like a deer in the headlights as far as women were concerned. Detaching from Gail took strength. You are strong. Your friends admire your loyalty. Loyalty and commitment come from inner strength. You can't manufacture that strength; it's a Gift.

"Evie stirred your imagination, but eight weeks, eight weeks of silence, and handsome young men can turn her head and her heart.

"John, what about the silence I endured? We met; we talked. I noted that you were passionate about your wife's memory and your daughter's life. I enjoyed the silence because I used it to know you more completely.

"So I decided in a glorious moment of whimsy that if I were

to really know you, I'd better know you. I had a rough idea of when you'd be home. I came by and pitched a tale to your housekeeper. She let me in. I found your itinerary and a spare key."

"Lilly, I feel you're describing some sort of illusion."

"No, illusions don't do for me what you do for me."

"What do illusions do for you?"

"Sometimes they make me feel quite foolish."

"Do you think Evie was an illusion?"

"I believe Evie fell for an illusion. I doubt if she would have wanted to sleep with a man who smelled of stale camel spit and bad incense."

"Good grief, I wasn't that bad, maybe a bit ripe."

"Overripe."

"What's that got to do with an illusion?"

"It shatters it. Men and women marry illusions. Learned authors write about man projecting an image of himself onto the woman who captivates his imagination, falling in love not with the object of great affection, but rather the illusion of what he projects onto the woman. Women do the same thing. Once the priest, minister, pastor or rabbi says, 'You may now kiss the bride', the illusion shatters. It's easy to fall in love with an illusion, difficult to love the reality of whom each really is."

"Have to agree with you. Marriages like my parents' marriage—loving, exciting, falling-in-love-every day marriages—

are honest, talk-about-anything marriages. The pastor has said it's the duty of a good wife to point out her husband's defects, and the husband's responsibility to honor his wife. In an ideal world there would not be any divorces, but the world and life are far from ideal."

John took a long look at this beautiful woman who had suddenly appeared in his life. "Lilly, what kind of an illusion are you?"

She smiled. "What you see is what you get."

About the Author

William Flagg Magee was born in Reno, Nevada. He was educated in Boarding Schools in the East and graduated from the University of Nevada, Reno with a BA in Far Eastern History.

Magee was in the financial services business from 1968 through 2005. Since then he has published *The Elephant Hunter* and under a pseudonym, Simeon Hoe, *Finding the Illusion*. Magee is also a photographer whose website is:

http://WWW.Q7PHOTO.COM.

William Magee has lived in Dallas, Texas since 1977. He is married. He and his wife have two grown sons. Prior to coming to Dallas, Magee lived in Reno, Nevada and Anchorage, Alaska.

His life has not been boring.

CPSIA information can be obtained at www.ICGtesting.com
Printed in the USA
LVOW06s1034071013

355740LV00001B/5/P